Ice Magic

Stories by Felicity Radcliffe

DEDICATION

To my dear friend, the late Chris Gunnell. An
excellent writer with a poetic soul. You will
never be forgotten.

CONTENTS

ACKNOWLEDGMENTS

As ever, I'm indebted to the many people who helped me write and publish this book.

Thank you, Val Littlewood, for designing another cover for me. You've worked your magic again with a gorgeous linocut image that is consistent with those you created for the Grand Union series – yet different. Your motif is brilliant too. You're a genius!

I would also like to thank the friends and family members who inspired some of the stories in this book. A pub conversation with ballroom dancers George Watson and Duncan Barritt sparked an idea that became Dance Away, and Pam Watson was kind enough to help me tell my rumba from my paso doble. Mike Hall revealed that a certain derelict canalside factory used to make hats – thus The Hat Factory was born. My husband Ian told me about Dillon, who stars in Dillon's Day Out. Lastly, my late father Don Radcliffe dined out for years on the incredible (but true) story that inspired Safe Landing.

My friends in Hunts Writers continue to motivate me. Special thanks to Georgia Rose, Angie Small, Evie Coppard and John Sissons – and particularly to Sally Runham, expert proofreader and critic.

Heartful thanks to my book club friends Maggie Tebbit, Jackie Digby, Ellie McKenzie, Rosalind Southgate, Julia Pearson, Sue Tebbit, Eileen Swanson, Janice Harding, Katy Smith, Emma Penniall, and Sarah Fussell. I couldn't do this without you, ladies.

A big shout-out to my wonderful colleagues and fellow scriptwriters at HCR104fm - especially Sue Rodwell-Smith, Jean Fairbairn, Helen Kewley, Tim Latham, Alice Goulding, and Fiona Ritchie.

Finally, I am blessed to have many friends who have become readers – and vice versa. I can't name you all here, but I'd like to mention some of you who, unknowingly, reached out to me when my confidence was faltering, as it so often does. Thank you, Elisabeth Payne, Christine and Nigel Fuller, Dorothy Bennett, Nikita Hirst, and Marie Busfield.

1 THE HAT FACTORY

It was an estate agent's nightmare. Never had Nigel needed to dissuade a client from selling a prestigious property. The penthouse covered the entire top floor of the converted hat factory and featured a stunning roof terrace, complete with outdoor kitchen and mammoth, party-sized hot tub. The indoor kitchen was a cavernous temple to industrial décor and the master bedroom incorporated a huge waterbed, whirlpool bath and walk-in wardrobe. There were his and hers washbasins in the ensuite, but the 'hers' basin was rarely used, and its toothbrush holder remained empty. Simon, the owner, preferred it that way.

Simon's property development company

had transformed the hat factory into luxury apartments and awarded Nigel the contract to sell them all, bar one. Nigel smashed the brief and cleaned up on commission, whilst Simon enhanced his already colossal fortune. In the process, mutual respect had turned into a sort of friendship, which was why Nigel could not stand by and let Simon sell the penthouse he had retained for himself. Not at a time like this.

Nigel prided himself on his negotiating skills. They had landed him the contract with Simon's firm and usually served him well, but today they appeared useless. He couldn't work out what was going on. Normally Simon was supremely logical, as befits a committed capitalist, but today was the exception. Today, something other than reason was driving him.

Nigel decided to give it one last go.

'Look, mate. Trust me. Don't do this. You know as well as I do that the market has tanked, on account of our government getting us involved in that poxy war in wherever-it-is. Bless their cotton socks. At least they had the decency to wait until I had sold all the apartments for you. Anyway, I digress. The market will recover, Si. It always does, you know that, but in the meantime, you'd be mad to sell. Just hang fire for a year, then you can clean up. If you sell the penthouse now, you'll never make a profit.'

'I don't care about making a profit.'

'Who are you, and what have you done with my mate Simon?'

'I know it might seem strange...'

'Too right, it does. Look, Si – I know what you're worth, and I know you don't have to sell. Not unless there's something big going down that you're not telling me about. You're not in trouble, are you, my friend?'

'No, it's nothing like that. I have my reasons, Nige. End of chat. I'm sorry you won't make as much commission as you would if I waited...'

'That's not the issue, Si. I just don't want to see you make a wrong decision.'

'I'm not. It's the right decision, but I can't tell you why.'

'I never had you down as a man of mystery.'

'I'm not, normally, but there's a first time for everything.'

'Alright, pal. I give in – but don't say I didn't warn you.'

Simon recalls the first time he saw the old hat factory. Its feet were planted firmly in the khaki waters of the canal and its red brick façade was studded with buddleia which had taken root in its crumbling cement. Each window had been shattered, presumably by missiles launched from the towpath opposite. Simon imagined how the panes would have presented irresistible targets to the local youngsters. Inside, pigeons ruled the roost. Their droppings littered both the factory floor and the machinery, which had been left in situ when the factory closed. The entire tableau was encrusted with grime and blurred by decades of dust.

If Simon had a poetic soul, he might have imagined, as he walked around the factory floor, the hats created in this venerable old building. The bowlers, once compulsory for businessmen, which were tipped politely when greeting a lady. The slouch hats used during World War Two, when they ran out of pith helmets. The fancy confections worn to theatres, cocktail parties and restaurants in a more elegant age. But Simon is not poetic. He has a good imagination, but it is deployed solely for commercial purposes. What he sees is a prime waterside location that, whilst derelict, appears structurally sound. He imagines how the windows, once restored and fitted with toughened glass, will flood the high-ceilinged apartments with light, ensuring they are fought over by upwardly mobile, style-conscious buyers. A basement gym, landscaped grounds and dedicated parking spaces will seal the deal. Simon calculates the return on investment and concludes that he can afford to create a huge penthouse apartment and keep it for himself. He imagines the ultimate bachelor pad. Then he gets to work.

It takes Simon five years to wrangle with the planning authorities, browbeat the contractors and drive the project to completion, but finally his vision is realised. The timing is perfect. The property market is booming, unemployment and interest rates are low and there are plenty of conspicuous consumers who want to boast of an address in this prestigious new development. Simon cashes in, then moves in. It amuses him to think that his customers, now his neighbours, imagine they are special, because they own an apartment in the newly converted factory, when in reality, they are nothing compared to him. He finds it satisfying that, in his penthouse, he is literally above them all. The king of his own castle. On his first night in his new home, he celebrates alone on his roof terrace with an ice-cold bottle of Krug. He traces the route of the moonlit canal, which scythes its silver way through the town and out into the countryside. He has never felt happier.

A few months later, Simon is crashed out on his waterbed. He often parties hard when off-duty, but this Saturday night was full-on, even by his standards. The occasion was the launch of a swanky new restaurant in Manchester, where the focus was on the clientele, rather than the food. The place was awash with models, musicians, footballers and the flotsam and jetsam of reality TV, plus a sprinkling of wealthy entrepreneurs like himself. Mindful as ever of his gym-crafted six-pack, Simon gave the elaborate cocktails a swerve and stuck to vodka shots.

As the evening progressed and the booze kicked in, lines were snorted with diminishing discretion. Overpriced canapés missed mouths, smashed to the floor and were slipped on. Simon rekindled an old flame, with limited success. They tried to make it in the ladies toilets but were too far gone to negotiate her shapewear. In the end they gave up, giggling, and did a line off the cistern, after which Simon decided to escape. It was all getting a bit too messy for his liking. He messaged his driver who was parked nearby.

Minutes later he was asleep in the back of the car. Maybe things would have turned out differently, had he left the party earlier. Or maybe not.

Simon does not like curtains; nor does he need them. It's not as though anyone can see in, and he loves the way the sun pours through the windows and skylights. There is no sun now, though. When he wakes, the windows are black. Simon cannot understand why he has woken. He always sleeps soundly, especially after a heavy night, and the penthouse is insulated from the outside world by elaborate soundproofing. All he can hear is the faint hum of the Sub-Zero & Wolf refrigerator. He closes his eyes and tries to zone out, but his head throbs from his earlier excesses and sleep eludes him. He curses as he remembers that he was in no fit state to put his customary glass of iced water on the bedside table when he got home. There is nothing for it; he will have to visit the kitchen and rehydrate. He sits up, then freezes, his headache forgotten.

The figure at the foot of his bed is translucent. The corner of the wall-mounted plasma screen is clearly visible through his torso. He looks straight at Simon and smiles politely, which cracks the dried blood that coats his face. His hair is plastered to his skull and his uniform hangs loosely on his spare frame.

Simon closes and reopens his eyes, but the figure remains, glowing faintly in the darkened room. Simon chastises himself for breaking too many of his rules at the party. In particular, he tells himself, he should not have snorted cocaine with his ex. As he recalls what they did in the ladies toilet, his thoughts go into freefall. Why didn't he stick to using his own nose candy, like he usually does? Leanne could have got that stuff from anywhere. She has some proper dodgy mates. Also, it could have been cut with anything - local anaesthetic, maybe even laundry detergent. That's why he's seeing things in the middle of the night. Either that, or she could have spiked his drinks in some sort of weird revenge plot – stop!

Simon tells himself to get a grip, banish the hallucination, grab some water and sober up. He tries to call out, but his parched throat can barely muster a croak.

'Alexa! Turn the lights on!'

The room remains dark. The translucent figure continues to stare at Simon. Then he holds out his right hand. In it is a grubby hat, the colour of the water in the canal below. Its brim is turned up on one side. Above the brim, in the centre, is a single, ragged hole.

'Can you repair this for me, mate? I copped a sniper's bullet in Burma.'

Desperate to be rid of his unwanted imaginary friend, Simon decides to play along.

'Of course. Just leave it on the chair.'

Instantly the figure vanishes. Simon smiles to himself and repeats his request to Alexa, this time in a slightly stronger voice. The lights come on, and he pads through to the kitchen for some iced water and a sleeping pill. When he wakes the following lunchtime, he barely recalls his bad dream.

Simon banishes the remnants of his hangover with a green smoothie, a bacon butty and a long soak in his outdoor hot tub. He whistles softly to himself as he returns to his bedroom to get dressed, a towel wrapped around his waist. As he opens the door to his walk-in wardrobe, he removes the towel and throws it over the back of his chair. Then he sees the hat on the seat of the chair and stops whistling. The brim is turned up on one side. There is a hole in the centre.

Simon lurches into his wardrobe and dresses haphazardly in mismatched clothes. He decides to take the hat down to the communal recycling centre, then reconsiders and tells himself to man up. He has never been one to sweep problems under the carpet. True, he is unaccustomed to encountering problems he cannot explain, but no matter. He decides to tackle the hat head on, as it were. A quick Internet search yields the contact details for a local milliner. He makes an appointment for the following day.

The milliner lives and works in a modest terraced house. The tiny front garden is crammed with bedding plants and two luxuriant hanging baskets drip water on either side of the porch. Simon knocks and the door opens almost immediately, as though the old lady has been waiting behind it. She ushers him into her front room. Ornaments clutter every surface, along with hats of all descriptions, in various states of repair. A ticket is pinned neatly to each hat. A fluffy cat is curled up on one of the velour armchairs. Simon's skin prickles.

The face of the milliner is scored and creased from decades of close work. The creases deepen when she sees the hat and smiles.

'Well, if it isn't one of those old slouch hats! Where did you get it?'

Simon ducks the question.

'What's a slouch hat?'

'It's a soldier's hat, dear. Our boys wore them during the war. Other countries wore them too. The Aussies were rather fond of them – but this one doesn't come from Australia. This is a local hat, no doubt about that.'

'How do you know?'

'They used to make them up at the old hat factory, by the canal. You know, the one they've done up all fancy? My mother worked there for forty years, and I followed in her footsteps. Until they closed it down, of course. So, I know what their hats look like, and this is definitely one of them. How did you come by it, dear?'

'It's a family heirloom, but I'd rather not go into detail if you don't mind. Let's just say it has sentimental value.'

'I understand. I suppose the hat's story is a painful one, given the bullet hole. I'm sorry for prying.'

'You reckon it's definitely a bullet hole?'

'I believe so. Did you want me to repair it?'

'Yes please. It would help my family a lot.'

'Then it'll be my pleasure. I'll make it as good as new. It'll help me as well. It'll bring back happy memories of my old mum – and the hat factory, how it used to be.'

Simon congratulates himself on deflecting the old lady's curiosity. Two days later, he returns to find she has delivered on her promise. The hat is pristine, and the hole has disappeared. He praises her skills, refuses her offer of tea and pays her a generous tip, praying he will never have cause to return to her cluttered house with its musty smell and clashing floral patterns. It makes his flesh creep.

That evening, he foregoes his customary glass of red at dinner and sticks to iced water. At bedtime, he places the hat on the chair, then settles down on his huge waterbed and waits for something to happen, but nothing does. No translucent figures, no voices. He tries his best to stay awake but eventually sleep claims him. When he wakes the next morning, the hat is gone.

After that, there are no further apparitions and soon Simon can once again sleep through the night. He feels mild irritation at an unsolved problem – he hates loose threads – but he refuses to dwell on it. Simon isn't the type to dwell, particularly as he is about to embark on a major new development project. It never occurs to him to share the experience either. Sharing makes him uncomfortable and besides, who would believe him?

The new development project is straightforward, compared with the renovation of the hat factory. Simon's team can handle most of the work and soon the boss is looking for a new challenge. He hears about a rundown country estate owned by a widow. Some digging reveals that she needs to sell in order to clear her late husband's debts, and Simon is ruthless. He turns the screws, negotiates a knockdown price and tells the widow she's lucky to sell at all in such an unfavourable economic climate. Then he goes home, hits the gym, eats a superfood salad and glugs a jug of iced water while watching Netflix. He's tempted to toast his success with champagne, but he has a busy day lined up tomorrow. Mind-altering substances will have to wait until the weekend.

The soundproofing throughout the penthouse ensures there is never any noise from below; neither from the apartments underneath, nor from the narrowboats which chug along the canal. That's why Simon is confused when he is woken by vague murmuring and shuffling sounds. It just doesn't make sense to him. He can't fathom how the noise has reached him in his insulated eyrie. He barks at Alexa to switch on the lights, then blinks as his eyes adjust to the glare. His throat is unaccountably parched, despite the copious quantities of iced water he drank earlier. He reaches for the glass on his bedside table, but it's not there. In its place is a note, which reads:

Go out onto your roof terrace. Look down. They're waiting.

Simon staggers through his huge kitchen. His legs will barely support him. He grabs frantically at furniture and appliances as he passes, to save himself from falling. Outside, the night is cool, and the moon is bright. Simon walks slowly towards the edge of the roof terrace, like a man condemned. He reaches the balustrade that surrounds the terrace and protects him from falling into the void. He looks over.

Below, the canal traces its silver, meandering, moonlit course, through the town and on into the countryside. Alongside, the towpath glows with diaphanous, uniformed men standing two abreast. The queue stretches into the far distance. It appears to have no end.

Every single person in the queue gazes up at Simon. Their expressions are hopeful, beseeching. Each man clutches a hat in his hands, and every hat is damaged. Some have only one bullet hole, like the one repaired with love by the old milliner. Some have two or more.

Many are riddled.

2 CLIMATE SUMMIT

She climbed the pinnacle, admired the view, and considered his marriage proposal.

Should she accept – or not? She couldn't envisage their future. She prayed for a crystal ball.

Black clouds appeared, thunder roared, and a boiling sea replaced the verdant fields below.

Clearly her quandary was irrelevant. Time to re-prioritise.

3 THE RED BUS

An icy wind blasted across Old Town Square, driving clouds of snow into the faces of the children hurrying home from school. Jana clutched her schoolbag against her chest, trying in vain to stop her coat from falling open. Her mother had promised to replace the missing buttons as soon as she had enough money. In the meantime, the winter snow always won and the walk home from school chilled her to the bone every day. Thankfully it took only ten minutes to reach the tiny house she shared with her parents and grandfather.

Jana pushed open the front door of her house. As usual it was scarcely any warmer inside than it was outside in the street, but at least she could escape the snow and the wind. Her grandfather, a bag of bones whose body was barely discernible beneath his winter clothing, was asleep in his armchair and did not wake as she walked through the door. Jana thought it was best to leave him be. She would follow her usual routine and do her homework while she waited for her mother to come home and cook dinner.

Jana carried her schoolbag into the bedroom she shared with her grandfather and settled down to her studies. She had offered repeatedly to help her mother with the cooking, but her mother had always refused. Education was a privilege that had been denied her, so she was determined that her daughter would not compromise her schoolwork by wasting her time boiling cabbage and potatoes.

Homework began with a Citizenship assignment. In that morning's lesson, the teacher had told them how much better life was now that the war was over, the Nazis had been defeated and the new government, called the People's Democracy, had been established in Prague, some fifty kilometres to the south. To Jana, though, life hardly seemed any different from the way it was before the war ended three years previously. Food and fuel were as scarce as ever, and her parents still had to work so hard just to survive.

Nevertheless, Jana thought, her family was more fortunate than many others. Her hometown of Mlada Boleslav, or MB for short, was where Škoda cars were manufactured, and the factory provided jobs for nearly every adult who was fit enough to work. Her father was on the production line for the new 1101 series, which had been launched earlier that year. He took real pride in his work, despite his modest wages. Her mother's job, cleaning offices in the main administration building, was monotonous and poorly paid, but at least it supplemented her father's income. At thirteen, Jana understood that there were people in other parts of Czechoslovakia who were struggling far more than them. It just didn't feel that way sometimes, especially in mid-winter.

Thankfully there was not much homework that night. Jana was one of the brightest in her class, so she finished it quickly and had some time to herself, which was a rare luxury. She put away her schoolbooks and took down a tin box from the shelf above her bed. A thin layer of dust had settled on the lid as she had not had time to look inside it for a while. Carefully she brushed the dust away with the sleeve of her sweater, so that the picture on the lid was clearly visible once again.

The picture showed a big red bus. Her Uncle Pavel, who gave her the box, had told her that buses like these could be found in London, the capital of England. Jana dreamed of going to London one day and seeing these shining, scarlet buses for herself. Realistically she knew that this was unlikely to happen, but her uncle had taught her never to let go of her dreams, as they were precious. When he gave her the tin, which was originally full of biscuits, he smiled and said that he knew the biscuits would not last long, but her dreams belonged to her and would last for ever.

'Fill your tin box with your dreams, Jana. Then hold onto them, no matter what.'

Jana did as he said. Into the tin went a locket on a silk ribbon, given to her by her father, plus notes from friends, pictures cut from newspapers and poems that she scribbled on scraps of paper. Over the years she filled the tin with verse. Some of the ink got smudged with tears after Uncle Pavel was killed in the war, but still she kept on writing. That night, before dinner, she added another short poem to her collection. Then she closed the lid and placed the tin back on the shelf.

Karolina and her husband José were excited to be moving into their new home on the outskirts of MB. Karolina's recent promotion to Senior Marketing Manager at Škoda meant that they could just about afford the mortgage. Money would be tight for a couple of years, but it would be worth it.

The unpacking seemed to take forever. Who knew that they had so much stuff? On the evening of day two, they finally got down to the last few cardboard boxes. José prised open one box and lifted the contents out one by one.

'Karolina – do you really need to keep this old tin? It's pretty beaten up – should I throw it out?'

Karolina glanced at her husband and shook her head emphatically.

'No – leave that one. My grandmother gave it to me just before she died. It has a lot of sentimental value.'

'Of course.'

José came from a large family in Valencia, so he understood the importance of family ties.

Karolina stared at the battered image of the red London bus on the tin lid.

'I'm glad you uncovered that tin, darling. 'You have given me an idea.'

The following Sunday, after she had finished packing her suitcase, Karolina searched through the contents of the tin box. She picked out a small locket dangling from a frayed, faded ribbon, plus a short poem on a scrap of paper. She folded the paper into a tiny square, placed it inside the locket and snapped the cover shut. Then she dropped the locket into her suitcase.

The sign outside the conference centre was written in letters that were taller than Karolina herself.

Škoda 2020

As she walked inside, Karolina felt proud to be helping to showcase the new generation of Škoda vehicles at the company's London conference. As she scanned the room, though, she spotted numerous things that needed to be fixed before the conference started at nine o'clock. Time to get to work.

On the evening before she was due to fly home, Karolina managed to get an hour to herself. She rushed into the tube station opposite her hotel and headed south on the Northern Line. She had been to London a few times now and was getting the hang of the tube network, which had seemed so perplexing to her on her first visit. Ten minutes later she got off at Bank, thinking that there would be plenty of buses around there. She was right.

Karolina waited at a bus stop near Bank tube station and got on the first bus that came along. As it pulled away she found a place on one of the long seats at the back, facing inwards. She peered anxiously out of the window, trying to memorise the route so she could retrace her steps after she got off. Then she delved into her pocket and removed the locket. Reaching up, she quickly tied the ribbon around the grab rail, then pressed the bell and stood up, ready to alight at the next stop.

'What are you doing?'

The voice came from the man sitting opposite, who had looked up from behind his newspaper and was frowning at her, clearly puzzled.

'Sorry,' Karolina replied. 'You must think my behaviour rather strange. The locket belonged to my grandmother. She dreamed of coming to London, but she could not. It was not allowed back then. In fact, she never left Czechoslovakia, as it used to be called. She is dead now, but I would like to make her dream come true. In a small way.'

'I don't think you're strange. It's a lovely thing to do.'

'Thank you – for understanding.'

Karolina smiled gratefully at the man, then got off the bus.

For the next two stops, the man wondered what to do. Eventually, he untied the locket from the grab rail, opened it and looked inside. The words on the scrap of paper made no sense, so he retied the locket in place and took its contents with him to his office.

'Alex – do you know what language this is written in?'

'Looks like an eastern European language, but I can't say which one. Polish, maybe? Hang on, let me Google it. I'll find out for you.'

Ten minutes later Alex reappeared at the man's desk.

'Mystery solved! It's Czech. If you want to get it translated, ask Filip in Accounts. He's from the Czech Republic. He should be able to translate it in seconds, as it's so short.'

When Filip read the poem in English, the man's eyes filled with tears. He picked up his phone and made a few calls.

Most of the people rushing along the London

streets did not notice the little poem that appeared on the side of so many buses over the next few weeks. They were too wrapped up in their own concerns for the words to register. A few of them did notice, though. The words of the short poem touched them and their lives, if only for a moment. The poem goes like this:

> "My dreams are just like little birds
> With golden clips upon each wing
> I know that they cannot take flight
> But oh, the songs that they can sing!"

Unknown author. Czechoslovakia. 1948.

Karolina never found out about the poem on the side of all the London buses, but that didn't matter. It was Jana's dream, after all.

4 A WINTER BURIAL

Snow fell as we buried my irascible mother
Ingrid, up north in Luleå. It obliterated her
gravestone, as if denying her death.

I fled south and returned in April. A woman
crouched graveside, scowling furiously at the
inscription revealed by the melting snow.

'I *hate* those words! Change them!'

'Sorry, Mamma.'

5 MEMORY SERVES

The interview was over. Felix thought he had answered the questions well, but the man opposite was hard to read. He leaned back in his chair and tapped his pencil against the leather in staccato bursts. Felix noticed that the left arm of the chair was tattered and worn, presumably from years of similar assaults.

'You pronounced my surname correctly, Mr Murray. That's rare.'

'I do my research, Dr Tchórzkowski.'

While conducting this research, Felix had discovered that 'tchórz' meant 'coward' in Polish, but he decided not to mention it.

'Please. Call me Anton.'

The doctor's glacial tone softened, just

slightly.

'Thank you, Anton. Likewise, call me Felix.'

'Your CV is excellent, Felix. Your references are exemplary. You have worked in top London hospitals. Clearly you are a well-qualified, highly experienced psychiatric nurse; therefore, I fail to understand why you wish to take a job in a small, obscure institution buried deep in The Fens. Enlighten me, please.'

'I'll be frank, Anton. Last year I volunteered at the London Olympics and fell in love with Joanne. By the time Usain Bolt won the one hundred metres, it was a done deal.'

'Quite the coup de foudre.'

'Exactly. The thing is – Joanne's a country girl. She farms part of the desolate landscape I drove through to get here. She loved the Olympic experience but hated London. It was clear that if I wanted to be with her, I needed to move, so I did. Then I proposed, and she accepted.'

'Congratulations. I predict you will be commuting to London within a few years. Meanwhile, the chance to employ someone of your calibre is too rare to miss. However, before we agree terms, there are some things you need to know.'

Felix decided to take the initiative.

'There certainly are. I admit I'm puzzled, Anton. By this stage in the recruitment process, I have usually taken a tour of the facility, yet in this case you appear to be making me a job offer without showing me my place of work.'

'I'm aware that our approach is unusual, but I regret to inform you that I cannot allow you access to Andrasta House until you have signed the Official Secrets Act.'

Felix listened intently while Anton explained that the residents of Andrasta House all suffered from dementia. Whilst their symptoms varied, they had one thing in common. They had all worked either for MI5 or MI6.

Anton leaned forward and stared at Felix.

'It's important that you understand. These men were loyal servants of the Crown. They would never knowingly divulge sensitive information, but sadly their judgement is impaired, so their discretion can no longer be guaranteed. Their careers finished years ago, so anything they say is no longer relevant in today's world and most of their references to their former lives are outlandish and patently false. Still, the authorities know they cannot be too careful. If you were to share some of the things they will tell you in confidence, as their trusted carer, it could...'

'Set hares running?'

'Precisely.'

Felix thought for a moment.

'I'm comfortable with signing the Official Secrets Act. It won't make any difference to me; patient confidentiality is in my DNA. I'm not James Bond; all I want to do is care for my patients. Where do I sign?'

That night, over a bottle of wine, Felix informed Joanne that he had just accepted the weirdest job offer he had ever received. He described his new post using the exact words that Anton had instructed him to say. Then he revealed his salary, which was far more than he had earned in London. Joanne raised one eyebrow; a gesture he found as tantalising as on that first morning in the Olympic Stadium.

'Sounds like hush money to me. Still, the extra cash will come in handy for the wedding.'

Security was discreet. The rustic sign at the roadside simply read:

Andrasta House. Visitors by appointment only.

Felix negotiated the gap in the hedge, which was just wide enough for one vehicle, then proceeded slowly up the driveway. Fir trees loomed on either side and stymied the weak winter sunlight. Ahead, a wooden gate blocked his path. As he approached, it swung open. He drove through and watched in his rear-view mirror as it closed behind him.

Anton waited at the top of the steps, next to the front door. Felix followed him into the cavernous, wood-panelled entrance hall. The institutional aroma to which he was accustomed was absent here. Instead, his nostrils were assailed by the beguiling smell of bacon, which receded as he climbed the sweeping staircase behind Anton, who told him that the residents had finished their breakfast. Some of them were relaxing in the morning room on the first floor, which was where they would begin.

As they entered the room a tall man, precariously thin, leapt from his armchair and rushed towards them. Like Anton, he wore a white coat.

'Robert! They told me you were coming, but I didn't believe them! I should have had more faith!'

Anton was firm.

'Now, Harry; we've been through this

already. This isn't Robert, this is *Felix*. Robert died in Bosnia.'

Felix stretched out his hand.

'Pleased to meet you, Harry.'

'Apologies, Felix. My mistake. Glad to have you on the team.'

Crestfallen, Harry wandered over to the coffee table and began perusing a selection of artfully fanned newspapers.

'Harry thinks he's a member of staff. We find he's much happier if allowed to wear a white coat, so I gave him one of mine.'

In the bay window overlooking a sweep of lawn, which sparkled with frost, another resident shuffled a deck of cards with the expertise of a Vegas croupier. His three companions watched, unimpressed. As Anton and Felix approached, the man looked up and beamed. Meanwhile, the card shuffling continued, uninterrupted.

'Good morning, doctor! Today is a *good* day! I am one hundred percent *lucid*.'

He began distributing the cards at lightning speed.

'I presume this is Felix, the new chap?'

'Correct, Nigel.'

Anton smiled down at Nigel as Felix extended his hand.

'Good morning, Nigel. Delighted to meet

you.'

'I won't lie to you, Felix. I have my bad days, but today isn't one of them. I won't give you any trouble. Not today.'

Anton and Felix continued their tour of the room. Anton made the introductions and Felix shook hands, committing names to memory using techniques honed over many years. The atmosphere was genteel. He almost expected to be offered Earl Grey served in bone china. Then, from a distance, came a series of urgent shouts. A nurse rushed in and whispered in Anton's ear.

'I believe Colin requires attention,' Harry called. 'Shall I see to it?'

'No, Harry. Felix and I will deal with this one.'

Anton ushered Felix down a long corridor. Through each door, Felix glimpsed spacious bedrooms. Every bed was neatly made, except for one. Colin yelled expletives as he destroyed his duvet.

'Colin became a lay preacher after he retired from MI5,' Anton explained. 'He'd be horrified if he knew what he was saying.'

Felix spotted an opportunity to demonstrate his expertise.

'May I handle this?'

Several incidents and many introductions later, Felix set foot in his office for the first time. Anton had long since disappeared. It was mid-afternoon and Felix had not had time for lunch. His stomach rumbled as he logged on to his computer. Already, he had paperwork to complete. He was trying to make sense of the digital workflow system when Anton appeared at the door with a tray of tea and biscuits.

'I'm impressed with how you handled today's challenging scenarios, Felix. You treated every patient with the utmost respect. You'll find they respond accordingly.'

Gradually, winter released its grip on the Fenland landscape. Green shoots pierced the black earth. Scarves were wound around necks in preparation for bracing walks in the grounds. Green-fingered residents returned to the greenhouses, intent on their seedlings. Harry and Colin were among them. Felix dropped by one morning to admire their handiwork and administer medication. Harry beckoned him over and whispered urgently.

'Colin's having a good day, Robert. While he's occupied, I need to share some highly confidential information. You see, the residents tell me things that the world needs to know, and I'm relying on you to disseminate the intelligence. In particular, you must warn the Government about the viruses the Chinese are growing in their labs!'

Harry grabbed Felix's hands and stared at him intently.

'Promise me, Robert, that you'll tell the right people, before it's too late. Before the Chinese unleash havoc on the world!'

Felix fought the urge to smile at Harry's dramatic tone.

'Of course, Harry. I'll communicate the intelligence at the highest levels in Government.'

'Thank you, Robert. I knew my old friend wouldn't let me down.'

That night, Felix poured his fiancée a glass of Merlot as they sat down to dinner.

'I wish I could share what these old dudes tell me. Conspiracy theory doesn't even begin to cover it.'

Joanne clinked her glass against his.

'What if they aren't conspiracy theories? What if those old men are telling the truth, and the Government locked them up to stop them from spilling the beans? What if...'

'Talking of beans, yours are going cold, babe. You're worse than they are. Let's change the subject.'

The weather continued to improve. Soon it was warm enough to open the patio doors that separated the ground floor sitting room from the garden. One afternoon, as Felix stepped out into the sunshine to check on the residents who were catching some rays, one of his feet slipped and he nearly fell. He looked down to see a playing card on the ground. Then another, and another. A trail of cards led across the lawn, then through a gap into the walled garden. His sense of foreboding grew as he followed it and found Nigel alone on a bench. Hunched over, his body rocked as he keened and sobbed. Felix sat down and put his arm around him. It was a risk; sometimes Nigel reacted adversely when touched, but not this time. When he looked up, his eyes were wet with tears.

'I knew you'd come, Felix. You're the only one who understands. Everyone else believes the nonsense they're fed on TV; that communism has failed and it's happy ever after. They think the Cold War is over when it has only just begun. Max Frisch had it right...'

'Max who?'

Nigel addressed an imaginary audience.

'What do they teach them in school, these

days? Google him, Felix – then you'll see they're all like Biedermann. They invite the fire starters into their homes and either ignore the petrol and gelignite or delude themselves into thinking the arsonists will never light the blue touchpaper, but they *will*. Mark my words. Felix, this is on *you*. If people like you, who have access to the truth, don't do something about it, you'll have no one to blame but yourselves. Before long, it'll be brother Slav against brother Slav, and that'll be just the start. Soon, everyone will pitch in, like they always do, and then...'

Nigel dissolved back into sobs. Felix gently put his arm around him and helped him to his feet.

'Come on, mate. Let's get you back to your room.'

'Can we pick up the cards on the way?'

'Sure, we can.'

Felix arranged to meet Joanne in the pub after work.

'You look tired, sweetheart. Hard day?'

'Kind of. One of the residents kicked off. He's a lovely old boy, but when he has a bad day, he gets really upset. It's a struggle to remain detached. Poor old codger. I do what I can, but it never feels like enough.'

'Oh babe, I don't know how you cope. Let me distract you; it might help. I visited a possible wedding venue today. It's pretty impressive. Want to see the brochure?'

'Sure. Why not?'

Felix agreed with Joanne's assessment of the venue, but even if he hadn't, he would still have acquiesced. To him, the wedding celebration was trivial; it was the marriage that mattered. However, he knew that his fiancée needed the fairy tale, so he was happy to oblige.

Looking back, he knew it had been the right decision. His wife treasured the memories of their special day and his twin daughters had loved looking through the wedding album when they were little. Nowadays, though, they lived through their phones, so Felix was astonished when, on their parents' tenth wedding anniversary, they retrieved the album from the bookshelf. As they leafed through the pages, they casually remarked that Joanne's dress was *'so 2014.'*

Their father's eyes brimmed with hot, unshed tears. Felix wasn't stung by their criticism; he accepted that his girls were now too old to be their parents' indiscriminate cheerleaders. He just hated the way his pride in them was eclipsed by fear for their future. He would give anything for them to grow up in a better world, but he and Joanne were realists. They knew it wasn't going to happen.

That night, over their anniversary dinner, Felix tried to silence the inner voice that plagued him night and day. The one that reminded him how, yet again, climate change had ravaged Joanne's crops and plunged the farm further into debt. The one that pointed out how years spent battling viruses and mental health crises in the NHS had turned his hair prematurely grey and scored deep lines across his face. The one that replayed the reports of potential short-range nuclear missile deployment in eastern Europe.

Joanne's voice brought him back to the present.

'Penny for them, babe?'

'Sorry...I was miles away.'

Felix raised his glass.

'Happy anniversary, darling. Cheers – and thanks for ten great years.'

'Cheers, babe. Any regrets?'

'You're kidding, aren't you? How could I regret marrying you?'

'That's nice, but what about...the other stuff? Anything else you'd do differently if you could go back?'

'How d'you mean?'

'What about work? Would you still have left that cushy number you had with those old spooks, out in the middle of nowhere, and returned to the NHS? Given everything that's gone down since?'

Felix thought for a minute.

'I reckon I would. Even in my darkest moments, I never doubted that it was the right call. I would have done some stuff differently though, while I was caring for the "old spooks," as you call them.'

'Like what?'

'I guess it's OK to tell you, now that so much time has passed...'

'Tell me what, Felix?'

'If I had my time over again, I wouldn't have changed the medication for two of the patients. Nigel and Harry, they were called. I put them both on stronger meds and increased their dosages. At the time I thought I was doing the correct thing, as they calmed right down afterwards, but now I'm not sure.'

'Don't beat yourself up, babe. Like you're always telling me - hindsight's twenty-twenty.'

6 THE NERD'S REVENGE

'You're an ugly nerd with tragic clothes and no friends!' they all said. 'No boy would date you in a million years!'

Yet, at the thirty-year reunion, bullies clamour for selfies. Men make discreet propositions. Bankrupts beg for loans.

Graciously she poses for the cameras, signs countless books, then leaves.

7 JOB SEEKER

Josh made a conscious effort to look away from his computer screen. Gemma, his manager, insisted on regular screen breaks, so he reluctantly followed the instructions she had issued via email. Josh doubted that Gemma was conscious of the irony.

Job Centre employees were urged to stop work every twenty minutes to stare at something at least twenty feet away for twenty seconds. That was how Josh noticed the man pacing back and forth outside, apparently oblivious to the nascent rain that pockmarked the pavement. As Josh watched, he halted outside the door, hesitated briefly, then crossed the threshold. Then he glanced over at Josh and their eyes met.

Josh's heart sank as the man walked towards his desk. His weekly report was overdue, but he reminded himself to put the customer first and forced a smile.

'Good morning. Can I help you?'

'I most sincerely hope so. May I sit down?'

'Of course.'

The man's tweed jacket was frayed around the cuffs. He shrugged it off and hung it carefully over the back of his chair, revealing a faded, but immaculately pressed pink cotton shirt.

'I require assistance in obtaining employment.'

Josh failed to suppress a smile.

'Pardon me for saying, but we don't get many like you in here.'

The man looked around at his fellow clients.

'It would appear not, although I understand that the service is open to everyone, even those of us whose wardrobes contain neither jeans, nor those ghastly hoodies.'

'Absolutely. Let me take some details.'

The man's name was Anthony Beauchamp. Once he was satisfied that Josh had entered his name correctly into the database, he gave his address as a flat on a notorious estate not far from the Job Centre. When asked what kind of job he was seeking, he replied that he would take anything. Josh glanced at Anthony's elegant, manicured hands, sprinkled liberally with age spots, and folded neatly in his lap. He made a mental note to disregard any opportunities in the building trade.

'Do you have any qualifications? GCSEs, apprenticeships, that kind of thing?'

Anthony smiled.

'Indeed. I took a first in Classics at Cambridge University.'

Josh sighed.

'Look, mate. If you're not going to take this seriously, I can't help you.'

Anthony was outraged.

'I am perfectly serious! However, I am also aware that there is limited demand for Classics teachers in the vicinity, hence my offer to take any available employment. The truth is that I am desperate. Perhaps it will save time if I explain why?'

'Go on, then.'

'Thank you. When I retired from teaching, my wife and I bought a beautiful bungalow in Devon. It was near the river, so I enjoyed fly fishing, and walking my little dog Homer along the bank...'

Josh seized at the chance to establish a

rapport.

'You a Simpsons fan?'

'No. I'm an Odyssey fan. Anyway, my wife Margaret and I led a peaceful, happy existence, until a day of unprecedented, torrential rain caused a flash flood that burst the riverbank and devastated our home. The deluge overturned the furniture and ripped up the carpets. When it receded, the smell was appalling. Almost nothing could be salvaged. Nevertheless, we would have recovered, given time, had I not omitted to renew the house and contents insurance. I used to handle all the household finances; therefore, it was my responsibility. We lost everything, and my wife never forgave me. She divorced me, emptied our bank account, and took little Homer with her.'

Perhaps it was the mention of his dog that caused Anthony to break down. Josh handed his client a box of tissues and gave him time to collect himself. Tears were a common occurrence in the Job Centre; they didn't make him uncomfortable. He stared out of the window at the rain, which had worsened, and was streaming down the plate glass windows. Eventually Anthony blew his nose.

'I do apologise. Permit me to continue. Margaret went to stay with a friend in

Scotland. Not long afterwards, I heard that she had met another man and moved in with him. He is rather wealthy, I gather. So much for nearly forty years of marriage. Meanwhile, I stayed with a succession of local friends; I believe the popular term is sofa-surfing. However, no one could put up with me for long. I had begun drinking heavily, and my behaviour was erratic. Eventually everyone's patience wore thin, so I moved to this town, and used my meagre resources to rent a flat in a rather disagreeable neighbourhood. It was all I could afford. Lonely and frightened, I began drinking more and more, until a few weeks ago, when I woke up in hospital. I do not recall being admitted, but apparently, I was found staggering around on the bypass. Luckily, some kind soul called an ambulance, and waited until it arrived, or I could have been killed.

Since then, I have not touched a drop of alcohol. The hospital referred me to a support service, and I am getting treatment. All I require now is a job. The rain washed my life away in a single day, but with your help, I believe I can regain my independence and my self-respect. Please give me a chance.'

Josh stared at the screen and tapped away at his keyboard.

'I think I've got something here. The DIY superstore on the retail park is looking for customer service representatives. You'd be working the till, walking the floor, showing people where to find stuff, and maybe providing a bit of advice, once you're fully trained. What d'you think? I know it's not what you're used to, but it's a start.'

Outside, the rain was easing off. A few pale slivers of sunlight forced their way past the clouds.

'That sounds perfect,' Anthony replied. 'I was always rather good at DIY. If you refrain from making any trite remarks about rebuilding my life, I'll be happy to attend an interview.'

8 FIRST IMPRESSIONS

The bridegroom was wearing sunglasses, which annoyed the vicar.

'Do you have the rings?' he snapped.

'My best man does.'

'Where is he?'

'Here.'

The dog lay at the bridegroom's feet. His pouch bore the Guide Dogs logo, plus one embroidered word:

RINGS

'Sorry,' stumbled the vicar. 'Didn't see you there.'

9 SAFE LANDING

The morning sun found a gap in the heavy, velvet curtains and instantly she was wide awake. On this momentous summer day, her first thought upon waking was the same as on every other morning. She simply had to move out – by the end of the year at the very latest.

'Annabel Darcy, you cannot begin the 1970s still living in your childhood bedroom,' she muttered to herself, padding across the thickly carpeted floor towards her en suite bathroom. As she filled the marble basin, she reflected that she would miss the luxury of her parents' Holland Park mansion. Far better, though, to slum it with a flatmate in Notting Hill or Bayswater and escape her mother's relentless crusade to marry her off.

Carefully Annabel backcombed her blonde hair, glued her false eyelashes in place and applied pink frosted lipstick. As she wiggled into her Mary Quant shift dress, she concluded that a trouser suit would be much more practical and comfortable for work. Alan, her immediate boss, would not object, but their fearsome Editor in Chief, Andrew Tilson, aka 'The Gaffer,' would not approve. He liked the women in his newsroom to 'show a bit of leg.'

As she walked into the kitchen her mother, Maud, wafted a languid hand towards the kitchen counter.

'Coffee is in the pot,' she trilled, 'and I have asked Betty to make you some food to take with you, as I know you're going to be late tonight. Ah here she is – thank you, Betty dear,' she said graciously, as Betty handed Annabel her lunchbox.

Annabel peered inside the box, then looked wearily at her mother.

'Ryvitas, Mummy? Again?'

'Yes – with cottage cheese,' Maud said firmly. 'A woman's waistline tends to thicken as she gets older – you need to have discipline to keep your figure! I know it's all beer and bacon sandwiches at that newspaper of yours, but you have got to say no, otherwise you will become stout, and no man will look at you!'

'Thanks for the lecture, Mummy, but I have more important things on my mind today,' Annabel sighed. 'It may have escaped your notice, but tonight a man is going to land on the moon for the first time. As Personal Assistant to the Picture Editor of a major Fleet Street newspaper, I am going to help put the images of this historic occasion on the front page, where millions of people will see them. I haven't got time to worry about waistlines!'

'Darling. You are a secretary who is staring thirty in the face, with no sign of a decent husband. Moon or no moon, the clock is ticking and if you're not careful, you will be left on the shelf!'

'Mummy. I'm only twenty-six, and the world is changing. I want more from life than walking up the aisle in a white dress and pushing a pram a year later.'

Her mother smiled and tapped the side of her nose.

'Pick the right husband, Annabel, and he'll hire someone to push the pram for you – you won't have to lift a finger!'

To Annabel's relief, their conversation was interrupted by her father, Aubrey, who rushed in, red-faced and flustered.

'Maud – I need you to help me find my new blue tie! Betty must have rearranged my wardrobe; I can't see it anywhere and I'm due at Westminster in an hour! The car's already on its way to pick me up. Morning, darling,' he finished distractedly, finally noticing his daughter and giving her a peck on the cheek.

'Morning, Daddy. I've got to go. Mind you don't lift a finger now, Mummy!' called Annabel cheerfully, shoving her lunchbox into her bag as she left the kitchen.

On the Central Line heading east, Annabel reflected on her mother's words. Maud's comments about her waistline had been forgotten, but four of her words - "you are a secretary" - had struck home. Annabel had hoped that her shorthand and typing skills, plus her excellent contacts, would help her break into news reporting, but all her efforts to land a job as a junior reporter had so far been in vain. She knew that she was valued by her own boss, but to his colleagues in the newsroom she was just one of the invariably attractive women who brightened the place up and performed the tasks that the journalists, most of whom were male, considered to be beneath them. As far as the hacks were concerned, she was fine just where she was.

Annabel's spirits lifted once she got off the tube at St. Paul's and took her favourite route to the office. As she turned into Fleet Street, she experienced the familiar sensation of being right at the centre of things – in the place where the news was gathered, embellished and packaged up for consumption by the eager masses. To be part of the daily adrenalin-fuelled frenzy of publishing a national newspaper was the biggest rush she had ever known, particularly on a day like today.

Briskly she walked across the crowded newsroom, which was full of men yelling into phones and marching around imperiously on supposedly vital missions. At the Picture Desk in the far corner her boss, the notoriously blunt Yorkshireman Alan Postlethwaite, sat in his habitual fug of cigarette smoke, poring over a transparency on a lightbox.

'Post has just arrived,' Alan muttered gruffly by way of a greeting, indicating a teetering pile of letters, newspapers and magazines on Annabel's desk. 'Sort it out while I'm in the Editorial Conference – then I'll brief you on today.'

Annabel watched as her boss wandered off towards the conference room, notepad in one hand, cigarette drooping from the other. She reflected that, despite his brusque manner, which some people wrongly interpreted as rude, she would much rather have him as her boss than The Gaffer.

'So, in conclusion,' Andrew Tilson barked at his editorial team, 'there is only one story that matters today. I don't care if the bloody Kray twins escape from prison – the moon landing goes on the front page. I want our coverage to blow every other paper away. Alan, I don't need to tell you that your pictures are key to making this happen. Do *not* balls this up. Right, that's it – bugger off, all of you, and get to work! Yes – Janet?'

The Gaffer folded his arms and glared at his Fashion Editor, who had raised her hand.

'We haven't talked about the angle I'm taking,' Janet began. 'I've put together a piece on futuristic, space age outfits...'

'I don't give a rat's crap about your space age outfits!' yelled Tilson. 'Just write whatever shit you women like to read about – and leave me alone!'

'If you don't care about my work,' shouted feisty Janet in her carefully cultivated Cockney accent, 'then why do you invite me to the Editorial Conference?'

'I don't know why I employ you, let alone

allow you in this room!' roared The Gaffer. 'Now get out of here before I fire your bony arse!'

Knowing when to cut and run, Janet hastily left the room.

Alan finished briefing Annabel, then reached for his phone.

'Right – I need to call the agency and find out when they're wiring the pictures through. Pop out and get me forty No.6 and a bacon sandwich, would you? Get one for yourself too – it's going to be a long day.'

'Thank you, Alan – I'm ravenous!'

Annabel grabbed her purse and headed off to the café and the corner shop.

When she returned, Alan was sitting at his desk looking terrified, his face deathly pale. Pushing his bacon sandwich to one side, he lit up and exhaled a despairing plume of smoke in Annabel's direction.

'Whatever is the matter, Alan?' enquired Annabel.

She had never seen her boss look frightened before. "Scared o' nowt, me," he had boasted on numerous occasions, particularly after several pints of best bitter. This time was clearly different.

'I just got off the phone to the agency,' he

began. 'Their cameras are down – a major technical malfunction, whatever the sodding hell that's supposed to mean. The upshot is that they will unfortunately be unable to wire us the photographs of the moon's surface that we need to put on the front page of our fine newspaper this evening, on pain of death. So, you and I, my dear, need to hit the phones right now and hire another agency, otherwise we are finished.'

Alan handed Annabel a crumpled piece of paper covered in hastily scribbled names and phone numbers.

'I suggest you get dialling and use all that posh charm of yours, to work us a miracle.'

An hour later, it was clear that the miracle was not going to happen. All the other agencies had signed exclusivity agreements with the paper's Fleet Street competitors, so there was no way to obtain the close-up photos of the moon that The Gaffer was expecting.

'So, what do we do now, Alan?' asked Annabel.

'What *I* do right now,' Alan sighed, 'is go and see Andrew Tilson, explain what has happened and fall on my sword. Then, after he has fired both of us, we go to El Vino's for lunch, get roaring drunk and afterwards leave

Fleet Street for ever. You go off and marry some chinless wonder and I spend the rest of my days taking pictures of fêtes for the Batley Chronicle.'

Annabel thought about lunch at El Vino's and suddenly had an idea.

'Alan – wait a moment – don't do anything hasty.'

Grabbing her lunchbox from her bag, she opened it and pointed to the contents.

'See these Ryvitas?'

'Never eaten the buggers, but yeah,' Alan growled. 'What's your point?'

'If you look closely, you will see that they have these little sort of craters on the surface,' Annabel explained. 'I thought that, if we could get our own cameras on them, blow them up a lot and perhaps get the art department to do some work on the result, then with a bit of luck...'

'...they'd look like the craters of the effing moon?'

Alan stared at her, his face a picture of incredulity. Then he laughed.

'Annabel, you're a bloody genius! I think you might just have saved both our jobs. Let's give it a try – but not a word to anyone, mind...'

Later that night, the first edition of the next day's paper went to press and Andrew Tilson, in a rare display of geniality, walked around the newsroom to congratulate his editorial team.

'Great job, Alan,' he beamed. 'Your pictures were outstanding! The quality was much better than I expected.'

'Thanks, Andrew. I couldn't have done it without Annabel, though.'

Alan pointed towards his secretary, who was picking up her bag ready to leave.

'Oh – you mean your posh dolly bird?' laughed Tilson. 'Best you take her to the Cheshire Cheese for a few drinks, if she has done a hard day's work.'

'Actually, I think she deserves more than that, by way of a reward,' ventured Alan. 'To be frank, she's wasted as my secretary. In my opinion she's worthy of a promotion.'

'Fair enough. It's good timing, in fact. One of the girls on the Fashion Desk has gone and got herself pregnant, so there's an opening there, working for Janet. She's a good-looking girl, your secretary; she'll fit right in. We can easily find you a new secretary to replace her. Can't say fairer than that, can I? You crafty old sod, Postlethwaite – catching me while I'm in a good mood!'

With that, the two men smiled at each other, shook hands firmly, then headed off to the pub.

'The Fashion Desk? That sounds rather nice, darling.'

Maud smiled at her daughter, who was sitting opposite her at the kitchen table.

'Will the designers give you any free samples? Do let me know if they have anything in my size – but none of those dreadful hippie kaftans, please. They won't do at all!'

'I don't care about fashion – or free samples. I want to be a news reporter,' Annabel retorted through gritted teeth.

Her mother, though, was oblivious, immersed once again in her copy of Harper's Bazaar. Sighing deeply, her daughter opened the evening paper and turned straight to the Lettings section.

Author's Note

The bit about the Ryvitas is true. A newspaper really did put a picture of a Ryvita on its front page and pass it off as the surface of the moon. Back in 1969 technology was limited, so they had to improvise.

The rest of the story is a product of my imagination, although a fictional version of a certain household name does make a cameo appearance. She used to work with my father when she first started out in national newspapers.

My late father was a Fleet Street journalist for more than twenty years. He also used to deliver lectures to police forces and schools on journalism and press relations. At every lecture he would place a packet of Ryvitas on the desk in front of him, to remind the audience not to believe everything they read in the papers.

Fake news is nothing new.

10 THE FUTURE'S BRIGHT, NOT TIGHT

My prom dress was way too small.

'Slim into it!' urged my ascetic friend. 'You've got time!'

I ignored her, grabbed my scissors and fashioned my dog a new coat.

Then I tore up my invitation, became a plumber, and trousered a fortune.

I don't own a single dress, nowadays.

11 A WOMAN SCORNED

My name is Diana. It means many things: luminous, divine, fertile, perfect. Once Tom would have used those words to describe me. He chooses different words now, but I don't. I still call him my husband, not my ex. I'll never refer to him that way. Marriage is for life.

Tom and I met at college. I was the clever one, whilst he was charming and streetwise, which counted for much more. He conquered the Square Mile, and made millions, whilst I quit my publishing career after a fight with my boss. I told her I didn't need the money and went home to get pregnant.

I built a gracious home for Tom and gave birth to Jonathan, our beautiful son. We both adored our child and looked forward to adding to our family. Tom loved teaching his boy to play football at weekends on the spacious lawn of our Surrey home. Nevertheless, I knew he dreamed of taking a little girl to ballet classes, and I resolved to make his dream come true.

One decade, two miscarriages and three rounds of IVF later, my husband called time. Apparently, I was no longer the beautiful bluestocking he had idolised in college. His City colleagues were all trading their wives in for younger models who thought they were masters of the universe, but I never imagined Tom would leave his son. I was wrong. She came along and turned his head. Suddenly, he was content to be a weekend dad.

'She' is called Inessa. Her name means 'chaste' - which is hardly appropriate. I would laugh, had she not destroyed my life. The woman is every wife's nightmare: coltish legs, full lips, tiny waist, and lustrous skin. Her body fat percentage is fashionably low and her tawny mermaid tresses artfully dishevelled. When I followed my husband along Bishopsgate one evening, and saw him greet her with a tender kiss, I knew my parents had given me the correct name. Diana – the goddess of hunting. I fixed my eyes on my quarry and vowed never to quit.

Tom wasted no time in building a new life for himself and Inessa – right on my doorstep. He blew his bonus on a large house just a few miles away from our family home in Surrey, where I still live. This allowed him to remain part of our social circle, and the number of invitations on my noticeboard declined sharply. People I had considered good friends apparently preferred to spend time with Traitorous Tom and his vile floozy than with me, a woman scorned, so I cut them out of my life. I don't miss them.

My husband's adultery moulded me into a different creature, but it was Jonathan who broke my heart. You see, my son liked Inessa. He knew how much I hurt, yet he returned from his access visits with cheery tales of the fun they had together. When I looked at his phone, found their 'family' WhatsApp group, and saw the photographs of them laughing, hugging, and playing, my resolve deepened. I would not lose my son to that woman. She had to go.

I followed Inessa everywhere. It wasn't difficult. She didn't work and spent her weekdays floating blithely between the gym and various restaurants and cafés. Soon, a pattern emerged. Her gym sessions were regular as clockwork, and every Thursday afternoon she would drive up to Box Hill for a hike. One sunny afternoon, I watched from the undergrowth as she sat on a bench, swigged from her water bottle, and took in the stunning views over the Surrey countryside. I realised then that I had my quarry in my sights.

The online car mechanics' course was described as "self-paced" - and my chosen speed was lightning fast. I blitzed through it in two weeks, then bought the necessary tools. When I checked the weather forecast for the following Thursday, I saw that heavy rain was predicted. Perfect.

I didn't follow Inessa that day; there was no need. By then I knew exactly when she would pull into the car park. As I engaged a low gear and began the steep, twisting climb to the top of Box Hill, I knew that she should already have left her vehicle and embarked on her hike. I hoped the rain hadn't put her off, but I needn't have worried. Inessa didn't keep a figure like hers by reneging on her exercise commitments. I sighed with relief as I saw her car, rain-drenched and unoccupied. There were few other cars in the car park, and no sign of their owners.

I donned my surgical gloves and wriggled

under Inessa's car. I had committed to memory the diagram showing where the brake pipes were located. For a moment I hesitated, then smiled as I cut them.

As I emerged, I heard voices. Walkers were approaching. I had planned to put the tools in my boot, to be disposed of later, but there was no time. Instead, I ran uphill towards the vantage point from which I planned to observe Inessa's precipitous descent.

My hiding place was further away than I thought. I was panting by the time I arrived. As I concealed myself in the trees, my phone pinged.

'Hi Mummy. Don't pick me up from chess club 2day. Inessa asked me 2 go 2 Box Hill Café, so I've skipped chess. She doesn't fancy hiking cuz it's wet and we like their cake. Don't be cross. Daddy will bring me home. CU later love Jonno.'

My sobs tore at my burning lungs as I flung myself downhill. I slipped on the sodden grass and heard a sharp crack as I fell, but a surge of adrenaline extinguished the pain and propelled me upright and onward, limping heavily. Below, the car park came into view. Two figures in hooded waterproofs climbed into Inessa's car and shut the doors, oblivious to my screams. The driver accelerated away

towards the downhill switchbacks.
    The hunt was over.

12 DIVINE INTERVENTION

His inbox bulged with unread emails. The television blared. His smartphone pinged incessantly. He prayed for the world to stop.

A TV announcer interrupted the programme. Due to the energy crisis, an emergency power cut would begin in twenty minutes - duration unknown.

He thanked God for His rapid response.

13 RECIPE FOR A DISASTER

Lisa stared across the kitchen table at her daughter Kate. There was nothing left to say. It was impossible to console a girl who had been forced to cancel her eighteenth birthday party and didn't know when she would next see her friends - or her new boyfriend. Kate had asked her to make chocolate brownies to cheer her up, but Lisa didn't have the right ingredients and couldn't even nip to the supermarket. It was closed due to restricted opening hours and anyway, there was no guarantee she'd be able to buy what she needed, even if it were open. Lisa reflected that coronavirus made it really difficult to be a mum to a teenager, which wasn't easy at the best of times. Then she had an idea.

When Lisa suggested trying her grandmother's recipe for rock cakes, instead of chocolate brownies, Kate was predictably unimpressed. She was even less keen when Lisa asked her to retrieve Grandma's ancient recipe book from a box of mementos in the attic, but her mother stood firm, insisting that it was a five-minute job. She could tell Kate exactly where the book was, as she had lent it to a friend who had been planning to open a vintage tearoom and had only recently put it back in the box, after her friend returned it. Eventually Kate gave in and stomped out of the kitchen, complaining that rock cakes sounded horrible and the dust in the attic would give her an even worse cough than this stupid virus.

Kate climbed up the steep steps that led to the attic. As she pushed her way into the cold, damp roof space, a spider's web caught on her jumper, and she swore under her breath. Annoyingly, the recipe book was exactly where Mum said it would be. Why was she always right about everything? Then, as she picked up the recipe book, Kate noticed a second book underneath, partially concealed by a battered carriage clock. On the cover was a single word – DIARY. Kate pulled the book out from beneath the clock and opened it.

Half an hour later, Kate walked back into the kitchen. When her mother asked for the recipe book, she realised she had forgotten all about it and left it behind in the attic. Ignoring Lisa's complaints, Kate showed her the diary she had found, held open at the page she wanted her mother to see. She remarked on what beautiful, ornate handwriting her great grandmother had, and Lisa explained how nearly everyone used to write like that in those days. Then mother and daughter sat down together and read the words written on the page.

"February 7th, 1919. Truly the weather has been atrocious these past days; bitter cold and stormy, with a leaden grey sky that precisely matches my mood. As I struggled into town yesterday, with my skirts whipping around my ankles, I noticed once again how few young men walk our streets. It really is too cruel. It was heart-breaking enough to see my friends lose their brothers in the Great War, and for our little family to mourn the loss of my cousins, Alfred and Frank, but this latest blow is almost insupportable. Influenza does not discriminate; it preys equally upon men, women and children, but to see it take men who survived the four-year horror and returned from the trenches, only to die young in their own beds, is tragic in the extreme.

And yet, amidst all this suffering, I must confess to a selfish and petty concern. I promised to reveal my innermost thoughts to you, dear diary, so I cannot conceal it from you. My concern is this. Whom am I to marry? Almost all the dear young men with whom I grew up are gone and of the remainder, a good number are afflicted with influenza, so could also be lost. I am nearly eighteen, on the brink of life, but in these awful times, life appears a poor thing indeed."

As they reached the end of the page, Kate looked up at her mother with tears in her eyes and said she didn't realise that people died from 'flu, back then, so Lisa explained about the influenza pandemic that came hard on the heels of the First World War and killed millions worldwide. Then she shared with her daughter some happy memories of her grandmother, the diary writer the same age as Kate who had put their personal coronavirus challenges into perspective and who did, eventually, find somebody to marry.

After Kate had gone to bed, Lisa sat down at the kitchen table with a bottle of wine and raised a glass to her grandmother, the writer of the diary she deliberately intended her daughter to find.

14 FLIGHT RISK

Airline passengers streamed into Arrivals, seeking signs bearing their names.

One read:

The World's Most Beautiful Woman

'Here I am,' said the beautiful woman to the man with the placard.

'No,' he replied, confused. 'There must be some mistake. You're not my wife.'

'She sent me instead,' the woman said.

15 DANCE AWAY

Summer always lies, but every year, we forget its treachery. In Bowford, a mill town bisected by the canal and brooded over by peaks and clouds, dreams of hazy, crazy days, nurtured in a triumph of hope over meteorology, have been washed away by the relentless rain. The sky is leaden, and the temperature struggles to reach fifteen degrees, even at midday.

Many of the dancers at Bowford Ballroom Academy have escaped to the sun, but Jean and June have stayed behind. The years have taught them to keep their powder dry, so they will wait until the schools go back and the Indian summer kicks in, providing a window of opportunity to bask in staycation sunshine before they dig out their waterproofs and count down the weeks until their winter cruise.

Jean and June met in primary school and have been inseparable ever since. Together they have experienced everything a hometown life has to offer. Furtive first kisses and fumbles under canal bridges, after the school disco. The satisfaction and tedium of long marriages contracted early. Children who have gladdened and broken their hearts in equal measure. Modest wages earned in humdrum part-time jobs. Friends who have come and gone, leaving shallow footprints on lives lived at an even tempo.

This is why they dance. For two hours each week they get to hit the accelerator, rip aside the grey veil and bask in glorious, sequinned technicolour. It's not about the costumes, though, as Jean always says. The fancy outfits are for competitions only and, anyway, they are merely the icing on the cake that is good technique. Preordained steps, honed to perfection by years of practice – that's what dancing is all about. You need dogged determination to be a good ballroom dancer, Jean reminds anyone who will listen, then reflects that if this were the only success criterion, she and June would win Strictly Come Dancing hands down. If there's one thing their lives have taught them, it's how to persevere.

Jean and June dance together, as a couple. They are not the only ones; Bowford Ballroom Academy boasts a number of long-standing female partnerships. In the early years, Jean and June begged their husbands to come along, only to be told repeatedly that 'real men don't dance.' Eventually they gave up and resigned themselves to dancing with each other. Each autumn, they listen as their real men deride the chiselled cheekbones and sculpted abs of the male professionals on Strictly Come Dancing. Then they watch them zip up the bomber jackets that strain across their beer bellies and head down to the local pub.

At Bowford Ballroom Academy, the other dancers look up to Jean and June. Their nimble quickstep is remarkable given that both are long-time Slimming World devotees who have never quite reached their target weight, and their fluid foxtrot is the envy of those half their age. They glide through the Viennese waltz with the apparent ease of the diligent, and their footwork is second to none. However, they are the first to agree that two dances elude them.

Try as they might, they simply cannot

master the rumba, nor the paso doble. Both women find it impossible to convey the sensuality required for a convincing rumba, when in the arms of their best friend. Nor can they summon the passion and arrogance needed for the paso doble. When June starts up with the stomps and the flamenco footwork, Jean thinks she looks as though she's annoyed at her children for being late for tea. She has a job not to burst out laughing, and she knows June feels the same way about her. The friends have discussed it and agreed there's nothing they can do. These two dances will forever remain outside their repertoire. They can think of few things in life that are impossible to achieve without a man but are forced to conclude that the rumba and the paso are among them.

The disappointing summer weather cannot dispel the chill that pervades the dance hall. Jean and June arrive early and decide to keep their cardigans on until after the first dance, by which time they should have warmed up. The other couples obviously feel the same way; hoodies and fleeces are the order of the evening, rather than the crop-tops favoured by the Strictly contestants in rehearsal.

Mrs Fry, their dance teacher, bustles in and collects the weekly subscriptions. The dancers all call her Mrs Fry, rather than Caroline, and she does nothing to discourage them. Her default mode is dour disciplinarian but, this evening, something is different. Tonight, the dancers detect a bubbly thrill of excitement, fizzing under her stern exterior. When Mrs Fry takes to the stage, she does not need to tap the lectern with her baton like she usually does, to call for silence. Her audience is already agog, eager for the announcement they know she is about to make.

'Good evening, everyone. We're going to begin with the quickstep tonight, but before we do, I'm delighted to reveal that we have a new dancer joining us in a few minutes. Marco has just moved into the area from Chester. He has been dancing since childhood and he and his ex-wife have won numerous dance competitions. He's keen to resume his dancing career with us following his divorce, and I've thought long and hard this week about who should partner him. It was a tough decision, but I've decided that the best person is you, Jean.'

Jean's mouth drops open. She stares first at Mrs Fry, then at her friend and partner.

'I appreciate the offer, Mrs Fry, but what about June? Who will she dance with?'

'I've already taken care of that. As chance

would have it, Margaret's knee is playing up again, so June can pair up with her Derek until Margaret recovers. That way, both of you will have the opportunity to dance with a male partner for a change. Derek has already agreed, haven't you, Derek?'

Derek raises his arm to confirm. Jean spots the sweat stain and glances at June, whose resigned shrug tells her she has seen it too. Derek is always clammy, Margaret once told them, even at the lowest temperatures. Jean's heart sinks for her friend, and she wonders whether this Marco will be any better. Then the dance hall door opens, and she has her answer.

Marco inspires a reflex action among the dancers. Cardigans and fleeces are shrugged off, backs are straightened, and hair is patted, because this guy is the real deal. Tall, dark and lithe, with broad shoulders, snake hips and eyes like melted treacle. His smile greets every person in the room, but has a secret quality to it, which makes each woman feel singled out and special. Even Mrs Fry, who is normally impervious to such things, goes all daft and fluttery, but who can blame her? Single male dancers are like gold dust in the world of ballroom dancing, but single male dancers who look like Marco are game changers. With

Marco on board, she can take her dance school to the next level. Smiling broadly, she invites him to join her onstage.

'Good evening, Marco. I'm sure I speak for everyone when I wish you a very warm welcome to Bowford Ballroom Academy. We're delighted you can join us. Chester's loss is our gain...'

Jean cringes as Mrs Fry twitters. She braces herself for Marco's look of disappointment when he discovers who his new dance partner is, but the newcomer surprises her. Smiling broadly, he steps down from the stage and strides across to where Jean is standing. He takes her hand, raises it to his lips and kisses it gently.

'I'll be delighted to dance with you, Jean. Mrs Fry tells me you are among the best of a very talented bunch.'

Later, Jean and June agree that the hand kiss would have seemed cheesy and ridiculous, had Marco not been so gorgeous.

During the quickstep, Jean and Marco quickly find their rhythm. Marco's stride is longer than June's, of course, but Jean finds it surprisingly easy to adapt. Their foxtrot is also a triumph, and Marco showers her with compliments.

'Mrs Fry has been very kind, Jean, by

partnering me with the best dancer in the academy.'

'You might say that now, Marco, but lots of people are on holiday. You're bound to think differently when people like Eva come back.'

'Never! They say you can tell immediately, when you click with a dance partner, and I knew, Jean – as soon as we began the quickstep. You and I are made for each other.'

At this point Mrs Fry announces that the next dance will be the rumba.

'Prepared to be disappointed, Marco. Everyone agrees – my rumba is rubbish.'

To be fair, it takes a while – but not that long. Over the next few weeks, Marco works patiently with Jean. He encourages her to take a more sensual approach to the rumba and stirs in her the passion and arrogance needed to deliver a rousing paso doble. Jean steps onto the scales at Slimming World and is astonished to discover she has reached her target weight, without making a conscious effort. She digs into the back of her wardrobe, retrieves dresses she has not been able to fit into for years, has her hair cut into a sharp, chin-length bob, and starts wearing lipstick again. Her husband is oblivious, but June notices.

'You look ten years younger, Jean. Must be

the Marco effect.'

'Don't be daft – although we were right. It takes a man to deliver a decent rumba and paso.'

'Not just any man. Derek doesn't have the passion or the sensuality.'

'Would you want him to have?'

'Yeuch – no. Don't go there. You know, I'm almost looking forward to Margaret coming back – even though it means I won't have a dance partner anymore.'

'Don't say that, June. Mrs Fry will find you another dance partner – hopefully one who's less sweaty than Derek. She'll work something out.'

In the end, though, Mrs Fry doesn't need to do anything, because of what happens next.

Eva returns from her holiday in Poland.

Eva's real name is Ewa, but she changed it shortly after she moved to England from her native Kraków. She quickly concluded that people were unsure how to pronounce Ewa when they saw it written down, and she didn't want to create any obstacles to integrating with the natives of her adopted country. Particularly not at work.

Eva holds a master's in information technology and is Chief Technology Officer of a local manufacturing company. In the early days, she fought hard to establish her credibility, particularly as she was appointed in preference to several homegrown candidates who now report directly to her. It has been a long slog, but she has won the respect of her subordinates and fellow directors by consistently delivering on her promises. Now that her seat on the board is secure, she has finally permitted herself to switch off from work occasionally. Nothing relaxes Eva more than dancing, so she was delighted when a chance encounter with Elaine, who runs her IT Help Desk, revealed the existence of a ballroom academy in nearby Bowford. Elaine was keen to attend, and Eva agreed to accompany her.

That was two years ago. Since then, Eva and Elaine have danced together on a weekly basis and become firm friends. Eva mostly doesn't mind partnering another woman. Elaine excels at the cha-cha-cha and jive, and although the foxtrot and the quickstep were initially more of a stretch, the two of them can now compete with the best in the group. Unlike Jean and June, they can even produce a creditable rumba and paso doble. The only dances they cannot master to their full extent are those that require lifts.

It wasn't always this way, for Eva. Back in Poland, her dance partner was Tomasz, a local tree surgeon. Their specialities were the Charleston, the jitterbug and the Argentine tango – all dances which can be enhanced by the addition of challenging lifts, and Tomasz liked them as dramatic as possible. Although Eva was slim, she was also tall, so she was never going to be as easy to lift as the tiny dancers in the class, but that didn't deter Tomasz. He boasted that he had the upper body strength to lift Eva with ease, so he was never going to swap her for a smaller model. Why would he? Not only was Eva a good dancer; she was also his dance partner with benefits. They both wanted the same thing. No complications, no strings, no drama. Just great dancing and great sex.

Privately, Eva is forced to acknowledge that she misses both the lifts and the lustful nights that followed each dance class. Since arriving in England, she has remained celibate; as a company director, she has deemed it too risky to get involved with anyone at work, and the only other men she meets are at dance class. The fact that they are all spoken for is irrelevant; none provoke in her the reaction that Tomasz did. Even though she is not looking for a relationship, Tinder feels too impersonal, but Eva has begun to think that she ought to give it a go. She worries that her libido will shrivel and atrophy from lack of use, leaving her with a life that, whilst outwardly successful, feels half-lived.

Every summer, Eva spends a month with her family in Poland. She insisted that this mini sabbatical be written into her contract and is glad of the downtime, although it is not without its frustrations, most notably her mother's attempts to marry her off, compounded this time by the discovery that Tomasz just got engaged and is unavailable to hook up. She congratulates him through gritted teeth, then spends an enjoyable few weeks catching up with old friends, but once back in the UK, she begins working on her Tinder profile.

A malfunction in the company's billing system means Eva is late for her first dance class after returning. Normally punctual, she arrives full of apologies. Mrs Fry is unimpressed. Elaine, who also lives with the vagaries of IT on a daily basis, is more sympathetic and pleased to welcome her back. During Eva's absence she has been forced to partner with the flotsam and jetsam of the class. She relates her unfortunate experiences in a low voice as they take their places for the quickstep. Then she notices her friend's eyes have wandered.

'I wondered how long it would take you to spot him.'

'Who is he, Elaine?'

'Name's Marco.'

'Is he Italian?'

'Italian heritage. Comes from Chester. He just moved here, looking for a fresh start after his divorce.'

'And he's dancing with Jean?'

'Yes. She was the best dancer available at the time, so Mrs Fry put him with her and partnered June up with Derek, who's minus a partner as Margaret's knees are playing up again.'

'Poor June.'

'And poor Eva. I'm under no illusions, my friend. Mrs Fry would definitely have paired Marco with you if you had been around. You dance just as well as Jean, plus your repertoire is wider. Also, not to put too fine a point on it, you're younger and better looking.'

'Jean looks good, though. She has lost weight - and that dress is rather lovely.'

'You're right; she has given herself a makeover. Check out the red lipstick...'

Eva has no time to admire Jean's make-up, however. The music starts; it's time for the quickstep. Eva feels the dance begin to work its magic on her. Without consciously meaning to, she performs with particular energy and verve. Mrs Fry notices, instantly forgives her for arriving late, and calls out to her.

'Lovely work, Eva! Keep it up!'

The next dance is the paso doble. As the dancers prepare themselves, Marco glances over at Eva. For an instant, their eyes meet, and he treats her to his most winning smile, but Eva does not respond. She is already in character, her expression haughty and arrogant, chin lifted, body poised and focused. Marco turns back to Jean and reminds her to adjust her top line. Her shoulders are hunched, he says.

During the next dance class, Jean performs her best rumba ever. Her hip action has been transformed by her partnership with Marco and she oozes a sensuality that belies her years. Mrs Fry compliments her afterwards, but the praise is surprisingly muted, given Jean's rapid progress with a notoriously difficult dance. Jean can't put her finger on it, but something about her teacher's reaction doesn't feel quite right. If she didn't know better, she'd swear her teacher was embarrassed.

At the end of the class, Mrs Fry asks Marco and Jean to remain behind. Apparently she has something to say to both of them. She waits until everyone else has left before telling them how well they have danced together and how Jean's dancing has come on in leaps and bounds in recent weeks.

'However, Jean – I have decided to make a change. From next week, Marco will be dancing with Eva. You will resume your partnership with June, and Elaine will dance with Derek. Happily, Margaret is recovering, but she is still not ready to return.'

Blink, and you would have missed the look that passes between Marco and Mrs Fry – but Jean doesn't blink. She sees the silent 'thank you' in Marco's eyes, and the brief acknowledgement in the eyes of her teacher.

Years spent shrugging off her husband's thoughtless behaviour have made Jean a placid person. The red mist rarely descends, but when it does, its overwhelming force takes full possession, as it does now. When she speaks, Jean's voice trembles with rage, along with her finger, which she points directly at Marco.

'You put her up to this, didn't you? I saw how you looked at Eva when she walked in last week! You're despicable, Marco! You butter me up, telling me what a great dancer I am, then the moment someone better looking, slimmer and younger than me comes along, you drop me like a hot brick – and you, Mrs Fry, go right along with it! You're nothing but a coward!'

'No, I am not, Jean. Quite the opposite, in fact. I had a difficult decision to make, and I made it for the good of the academy. You know as well as I do that we have the regional championships coming up soon. I believe that together, Marco and Eva will give Bowford Ballroom Academy its best chance of getting placed in that competition, something we haven't managed to achieve for over a decade. We cannot afford to miss this opportunity. It's as simple as that.'

'So, I have to take one for the team?'

'If you wish to put it like that, then yes.'

'OK, I will, but you know what? I'll be happy to go back to June. I never asked to stop dancing with her in the first place. She's my best friend, and she knows more about loyalty than you two ever will! You can stuff your regional championships – some things are more important.'

Jean catches up with Marco as he walks briskly towards his car.

'Don't you dare dash off! You owe me an explanation.'

'I thought Mrs Fry explained it quite clearly.'

'Do you think I'm stupid? That stuff about the regional championships was a red herring. Admit it – you put her up to it! You asked Mrs Fry to pair you up with Eva!'

'Alright, if you insist – I did. Of course, I did. You said it yourself, Jean. Eva is prettier, much slimmer and a great deal younger than you. It was a complete no-brainer, to be frank. Look at yourself! OK, so you've lost weight and smartened yourself up a bit, in an attempt to be worthy of a partner like me, but it was never going to suffice. Your waist will always be thick, and so will your ankles. Despite the hours I spend doing bench presses in the gym, I'll never be able to lift you properly. How could you ever imagine I'd want to compete with you at the regional championships? You would look ridiculous in the costumes, and as for the stage make-up, are you familiar with the phrase "lipstick on a pig?" I believe it's appropriate, in your case. Have I made myself clear?'

'What you have made clear, Marco, is that you're no gentleman. Not like I thought you were, when you first kissed my hand. My mistake. I feel sick to think I ever let you put your hands on my thick waist, and I feel sorry for Eva. I hope she dumps you as nastily as you have ditched me. Now get out of my sight!'

Anger keeps the tears at bay until after Marco's car disappears. Jean is grateful that she managed not to break down in front of him. Thankfully, June's house is only five minutes' walk away, not far from her own. Jean knows that both their husbands will be at the pub; ballroom dancing conveniently takes place on the same night as darts practice. She will have plenty of time to tell June all about what Marco said and cry the pain away with the help of Prosecco and mini rolls. June always has lots of both in stock.

Later that week, she opens her front door one evening to find Eva standing there. Jean has no idea how Eva discovered where she lives, but then again Eva does work with computers. Maybe she is able to find this stuff out. She invites Eva in for a cup of tea, or maybe a glass of wine? Eva chooses wine and explains over the Pinot Grigio how Mrs Fry emailed her to say she wanted her to pair up with Marco in place of Jean. Apparently Elaine was not surprised, although Eva says that her friend is less than pleased at the prospect of dancing with sweaty Derek. However, it's Jean who Eva is most worried about. She wants Jean to know that she had nothing to do with Mrs Fry's decision. Jean believes her and tells her not to worry. Then she warns her to watch out for Marco. She refills Eva's glass as she reveals how wantonly cruel he is, under the suave exterior, but even as she speaks, she realises that she is wasting her breath. After all, the lure of the bad boy is as old as time itself.

Eva and Marco form an outstanding dance partnership. The chemistry between them is obvious, and they rapidly develop a wide portfolio of dances that they perform beautifully. To her delight, Eva is once again able to enjoy the Argentine tango, the Charleston and the jitterbug. She tells Marco about the lifts she and Tomasz use to execute during these three dances, and Marco practises them with her over and over, until he has them down perfect. It almost seems to Eva as though Marco feels compelled to compete with Tomasz, a man whom he has never met, but she doesn't complain. The results are outstanding, and she regards Marco's diligence as proof that he cares. She has never told him that she and Tomasz were lovers, but she doesn't need to. She knows that he knows.

After their second class together, Marco asks her to have a drink with him at the local wine bar. They each enjoy two glasses of Sauvignon Blanc, then move on to the Picpoul in week three. The following week, Marco remarks that it's a shame to limit themselves to two glasses each, just because they have to drive. Perhaps Eva would like to join him at his canalside penthouse apartment, to share a fine bottle of Pouligny Montrachet which he acquired recently from his wine club? He'll book her a taxi home. Eva accepts his offer. They both know he won't need to book a taxi. A few wine tastings later, she deletes her Tinder profile.

Once again Eva has a dance partner with benefits, and every aspect of her life is enhanced as a result. Work colleagues tell her she seems more relaxed, and her fellow directors praise her calm demeanour when hackers attempt to access the company's IT systems. The cybersecurity protocols instituted by Eva prove resilient, the company receives favourable press coverage, and the Managing Director pays Eva a substantial bonus. Now that her skills are widely known, he realises that the head-hunters will come calling, and he cannot afford to lose her.

Meanwhile, Mrs Fry asks Marco and Eva to take part in some private dance sessions, to hone their technique in preparation for the regional championships. Eva is happy to do so. More sessions mean a better performance on the dancefloor - and more wine tastings. Marco raises no objections and wonders why he took so long to divorce his high maintenance, demanding wife. If he had known how easy it would be to find someone like Eva, who does not wish to leave so much as a toothbrush at his house, he would have done it much sooner.

At the weekly dance classes, the progress made by Eva and Marco during their private sessions with Mrs Fry is clear to see. All the dancers at Bowford Ballroom Academy, even Jean and June, agree that the pair are destined to be serious contenders at the regional championships. As it turns out, they are wrong about this although, to be fair, what happens next could not have been predicted by any of them.

Dominique returns from her assignment in Brazil.

Despite her name, Dominique is not French, but she works for a French fashion retailer and speaks the language fluently. The company hired her as an ambassador when her modelling career was drawing to a close, and soon realised that they had taken on more than they expected, but in a good way. Dominique proved to have exceptional business acumen and was keen to be more than just the face of the business, so she became involved with Operations and was instrumental in opening the company's first store outside France, in neighbouring Switzerland. Over the next few years, the chain expanded rapidly. Dominique was initially deployed across Europe, then further afield, first in Asia and more recently in South America. During each foray into a new territory, she is typically overseas for several months. Upon her return home from assignment, she resumes her dance classes until she flies out to her next exotic location. Whilst she is away, she either finds a local dance class or diligently takes part in online tutorials. Either way, she is never rusty when she returns to Bowford Ballroom Academy. On the contrary, she always has new skills to demonstrate, and Dominique loves to show off. A part of her will forever remain on the catwalk. Recently she helped launch a network of stores in and around Buenos Aires.

Needless to say, her Argentine tango is to die for.

Having lived in London for most of her life, Dominique finds Bowford provincial and has dismissed most of its inhabitants as unworldly and small-minded. Country living is her labour of love; a sacrifice made for the sake of her wife, Heather, who was suffocating in the Metropolitan Police until she was seconded to one of the largest police investigations in northern England since the Moors Murders. Heather made friends with a group of officers who lived on the edge of the Peak District and ended up sofa-surfing on her days off, as Dominique was overseas, and she couldn't face the long journey back to an empty London flat. She fell in love with the area, and in particular with Bowford, whose converted canalside mills are home to coffee shops, art galleries, luxury apartments, health clubs and even a micro-brewery. Heather longed to return, but not as a police officer. Disenchanted by lenient sentences and plea bargains, she decided to retrain as a yoga teacher and forge a new life in a place where she could breathe.

Dominique voiced her misgivings but was ultimately supportive. Heather's happiness was her top priority, and she figured that her frequent overseas trips would allow her to continue her love affair with city living, in locations that offered the twin benefits of novelty and sunshine. She concluded that she was happy to close the book on London and relocate with Heather to Bowford, although she makes a point of returning to the smoke each year for London Fashion Week.

Diane was one of Heather's first customers. She and Dominique got talking during an all-day yoga retreat in Heather's new studio. Diane explained how she hoped yoga would provide her with the improved flexibility and focus needed to take her ballroom dancing to the next level. Delighted, Dominique revealed that she too was a dancer. Since moving to the area, she had not found time to search for a dance academy and thought she was unlikely to find one which would accept a sporadic participant. She explained about her job, and Diane said it wouldn't be a problem. She was sure Mrs Fry would welcome someone like Dominique with open arms. The only problem was that Bowford Ballroom Academy was short of male dancers. It was likely that Dominique would have to pair up with another woman. Would that be a problem? Dominique smiled at Diane, then glanced over at Heather, whose blonde hair tumbled forward as she demonstrated the Downward Dog to one of the other participants.

'I'm sure it'll be fine. My wife's not the jealous kind.'

'Your – your wife?'

Dominique watched as the penny dropped and Diane grappled for a response.

'But you don't wear a ring...'

'Heather does, but I don't. I'm not the ring-wearing kind. She's cool with it.'

'Oh – I see.'

Dominique's preconceptions about small-town minds were confirmed. She decided to join Bowford Ballroom Academy because she missed going to dance classes, but she did not expect to gel with any of the other dancers. However, time proved her wrong. She and Diane became dance partners, then gradually morphed into firm friends, and she found that she grew to like many of the other dancers too. Accustomed to the image-obsessed fashion pack, she found their lack of artifice a relief and admired their willingness to laugh at themselves. The ballroom academy became the perfect antidote to work. When Dominique returned home after each assignment, she was invariably excited to get dancing once again.

Dominique's return to class is greeted by squeals from Diane, who rushes over to greet her friend and dance partner. Dominique drops her bag to the floor and hugs her. The other dancers cluster round, eager to welcome the star pupil back from Brazil. Dominique soaks up the attention and graciously sprinkles her fairy dust in return for their adulation. Only one dancer stands apart, unaffected by the excitement. Marco watches, his expression impassive, as Eva slips her arms around Dominique's tiny waist and kisses her on the cheek, then stands back to admire her friend's outfit. He pulls a comb from his pocket, slicks back his hair, and waits for Mrs Fry to call the group to order.

'Quiet, everybody! Clearly we're all delighted to welcome Dominique back from Brazil, but we do have to fit in some actual *dancing* during tonight's session. It is lovely to see you though, Dominique. You appear to have brought some of the glamour of Rio with you – that outfit is stunning. We shall begin with an Argentine tango, in your honour, but first, can everyone please check the board? I've made some changes to ensure that Dominique and Diane can resume their partnership, which we know works so well. Marco, I've obviously kept you and Eva together, as you'll be competing in the regional championships in a few weeks' time. Indeed, most of you are unaffected, but there are a few adjustments, so please check before you assume your places for the first dance. Thank you.'

Dominique and Diane take a while to find their feet, which is only to be expected after months apart. However, a few numbers in, the magic is back. Dominique recalls how she once confessed to Diane, over a few drinks, that she sometimes imagined Diane was Heather whilst dancing, to lend credibility to the more passionate numbers. Diane had replied that she should be offended but wasn't. After all, she did the same thing, albeit with Ryan Gosling, rather than her own husband. Then they had both laughed, refilled their glasses and agreed that when it comes to ballroom dancing, the end justifies the means.

Looking back on that evening, Dominique realises they were right. Their ability to channel unrelated and, in Diane's case, unrequited passion for other people into their dancing has allowed them to create some of the most authentic performances ever seen at the academy, according to Mrs Fry. Nevertheless, despite the compliment, Dominique is not fooled. She realises their teacher is disappointed that she and Diane are the most gifted duo in the academy. Despite the introduction of same-sex partnerships in Strictly, Mrs Fry knows that the judges in the upcoming regional championships will favour a male-female pairing. The new guy, Marco, and the lovely Eva are in with a chance, but in a fair and truly diverse world, she and Diane would be the favourites. Dominique tells herself there is no point in feeling bitter, but she cannot help herself. The applause she received as she stalked down the world's catwalks in the finest designer clothes still has its hook in her. She craves the adulation reserved for a fantasy. Above all, she loves to win.

The following week, Eva wakes up in Marco's bed on the morning after their second private dance session in three days. Mrs Fry is ramping up the frequency as the date for the regional championships edges closer. The couple continue to improve. Last night they executed the Charleston and the jitterbug with near perfect precision, although something was off with their tango. Marco's normal intensity was absent. When Eva asked him what the problem was, he replied that he was simply tired after a long day at work.

TOGETHER WITH THEIR FAMILIES

ALEX

and

NEIL

INVITE YOU TO CELEBRATE THEIR WEDDING

JUNE | 8TH | 2024

2PM

BLACK HORSE, BASTON, PE6 9PB

BBQ+boogie to follow

WILL YOU BE JOINING US?

. . . .

WHAT SONG WILL GET YOU ON THE
DANCE FLOOR?

. . . .

ANY DIETARY REQUIREMENTS?

. . . .

PLEASE RSVP TO THE
QUESTIONS ABOVE BY APRIL 8TH
TO

turneradventures86@gmail.com

Gift
Wishlist

SCAN
ME

Afterwards they hooked up at his house as usual, but she couldn't help noticing that the wine Marco poured for her beforehand was from a supermarket value range. The fine vintages from his wine club were nowhere to be seen.

Eva grabs her overnight bag and heads for the bathroom. When she emerges half an hour later, suited and booted, Marco is awake. As he sits up, the duvet falls away to reveal his waxed, bronzed torso, sculpted to perfection in the gym. His physical beauty still makes Eva catch her breath. Familiarity has not dulled its impact. She's tempted to return to bed, but she has a board meeting at nine o'clock, so she'll have to pass. Not that Marco is offering. His 'come to bed' smile is noticeably absent.

'Eva, I need to tell you something.'

Eva's stomach flips. She knows that conversations which start this way are never pleasant, but she's not a teenager. She doesn't give away her power so easily. She squares her shoulders.

'Better make it quick. I have a board meeting. What is it?'

'It's Mrs Fry. She wants to make some changes.'

'What sort of changes?'

'She intends to move some couples around. Specifically, she wants to pair me up with Dominique – for the regional championships.'

'I see. So, that's one change. What other changes has Mrs Fry got planned?'

'Er...she wants you to dance with Elaine again – seeing as you're so good together.'

'I see. So, just the one change then. Requested by you, I suspect – not by Mrs Fry.'

'No, Eva – you've got it all wrong! You see, I...'

'Don't waste your breath, Marco! I'm not stupid. I'm a Chief Technology Officer and expert computer programmer. One of the most important skills in my job is the ability to identify patterns. It's not exactly hard for me to see that you've done the same thing to both me and Jean...'

'You're wrong, Eva. It's not the same as with Jean. You're nothing like her. You're very attractive, I love your company, and you're a wonderful dancer. It's just that Dominique is...'

'A stunning ex-model who dances like a dream and will give you the best possible chance of winning at the regional championships.'

'You're right, in one sense. It is about the

dancing – and nothing else. What I mean is – even though you and I won't be dancing together, we can still do – this.'

Marco smiles as he gestures towards the rumpled duvet, and Eva feels sick. She wishes she had spent more time in the shower – and scrubbed harder.

'I see, Marco. You'd like to retain the option of a booty call with me in case Dominique doesn't put out. All I can say is – good luck with that.'

Marco stops smiling.

'Really? Why wouldn't she? *You* did. Am I to assume it's over?'

'There's nothing to *be* over, Marco. Not like there was with Tomasz. You know, he was a better dancer than you will ever be, however much you practise, and do you know why? Tomasz is a *real* man, who doesn't feel the need to have his chest hair waxed in a beauty parlour. Who gets his tan, and his abs, from doing hard physical work in the hot sun, rather than performing bench presses and paying for his body to be sprayed with gunk. He is genuine, whereas you, Marco, are nothing but a fraud. You are like that Barbie boyfriend – what is his name? Ken! That's it! A plastic, fake doll! Also, you could have told me all this yesterday, to save me from having to spend another night between your cheap, synthetic sheets! You disgust me.'

Marco listens as Eva clatters down the hallway and slams the door. He feels sorry he has burned his bridges with her, but it can't be helped, and perhaps it is for the best. From now on, he will need to focus his attention solely on Dominique.

Margaret's knee is still not fully recovered. However, Mrs Fry thinks it is best to reunite Elaine with Eva, rather than keep her dancing with sweaty Derek. She feels it's the least she can do for Eva, given the circumstances, so she tells Diane that it's her turn to partner Derek, just for the time being. She promises Diane that Margaret will be back soon and anyway, she's used to pairing up with different partners in Dominique's absence, isn't she? She's sure Diane will learn something from Derek, and she will have the satisfaction of watching her dear friend Dominique progress. Maybe Dom will even lift the trophy at the regional championships! Diane realises that resistance is futile. She grits her teeth, takes her place in Derek's arms and thinks hard about Ryan Gosling.

From the outset, it is obvious that Dominique and Marco make sense as a couple. Everyone thought that Marco danced beautifully with Jean, and even more so with Eva, but with Dominique, he takes things to a whole new level. His interpretation of the paso doble is hugely expressive, and their rumba oozes sex appeal. Whilst she regrets the disruption to group dynamics caused by the recent changes, Mrs Fry is forced to acknowledge that greatness is seldom achieved without some degree of trauma.

During the break, Dominique spots Eva heading towards the ladies toilet and follows her at a discreet distance. She fiddles with her hair in front of the bathroom mirror until Eva emerges from the cubicle.

'Eva – we need to talk.'

'Sure.'

'You have to believe that I never asked Mrs Fry to pair me up with Marco.'

'I know you didn't. I didn't either. I said the same thing to Jean, after he rejected her, but I never thought he would do the same thing to me. I've been so stupid, Dom! Jean warned me that Marco was bad news, but I didn't listen. Instead, I danced with him, drank his wine, listened to his cheesy chat-up lines - and one thing led to another.'

'You slept with him?'

'Yes, I did – and now I wish I hadn't. At

least you won't have that problem.'

'Indeed not. Best chalk it up to experience, my friend. We all make mistakes in that department. I certainly have. One day, over a drink, we should share war stories. I'll tell you all about the times I got it wrong – including hitting on women who turned out to be straight.'

Jean emerges from one of the cubicles. Neither Eva nor Dominique noticed her come in. She smiles at them via the mirror as she washes her hands.

'I'm glad to see you two aren't fighting over Marco. I hope you don't think I'm being nosy, but I couldn't help overhearing your conversation, and it got me thinking. Dom – does Marco know you're gay?'

'I've no idea. It hasn't exactly come up in conversation.'

Eva hands Jean a towel.

'He hasn't got a clue.'

'How d'you know, Eva?'

'You just reminded me of a conversation we had when he was lying in bed, right after revealing he had ditched me for Dom here.'

'Classy.'

'That's Marco for you. Anyway, he said that even though we would not be dancing together anymore, we could still hook up – or words to that effect.'

Dom slings her arm around Eva's shoulders.

'What an utter sleazeball! I hope you told him where to go...'

'Of course, I did, but the interesting thing is – I remember exactly what I said. I accused him of wanting to retain the option of a booty call with me in case you didn't put out. Then I said, pointedly: "Good luck with that," and he didn't react the way he would have done, had he known you were gay. Quite the opposite. He just smiled at me and said: "Why wouldn't she? *You* did." Now here's the thing - I didn't enlighten him as to why you wouldn't succumb to his charms. I was too busy telling him exactly what I thought of him.'

'That's perfect, Eva. What an idiot that man is. Now listen, you two. I think we can have a little fun at Marco's expense. Dominique, we all know how competitive you are. You'd love to win at the regional championships, wouldn't you?'

'Of course, Jean – even though it appears I have to dance with a total lowlife to do it.'

'Needs must, I'm afraid. Now, Dom, what you're going to do is – let lover boy feed you all his lines, smile sweetly, and promise him jam tomorrow, as it were. Get Marco to channel all his passion for you into his dancing, so he turns in a winning performance at the regional championships. Then afterwards, we'll break the news to him in such a way as to humiliate him completely, just like he did to me and Eva.'

'How will we accomplish that?'

'Leave that to me – and June. My old friend can be quite devious when she wants to be – and so can I. We need to be, what with our husbands. Anyway, we'll come up with a cunning plan to make the regional championships a night to remember – in more ways than one – and in the meantime we'll make sure none of the other dancers spill the beans. It'll be a small victory, but a sweet one.'

In the weeks leading up to the regional championships, Marco and Dominique rehearse their chosen dance – the rumba – until their performance is innate. Both their muscle memories are sharpened to the point where a wrong step is unthinkable, leaving them to focus on stylistic interpretation, which they know will be the difference maker. At this level, their rivals are as unlikely as they are to put a foot wrong. They know that if they are going to win, they must light up their performance with genuine emotion and passion. Luckily, for Marco, passion is not an issue.

During every dance session, Marco showers Dominique with compliments. He tells her that she is the most beautiful, elegant woman he has ever encountered and repeatedly invites her to join him for a drink at his favourite wine bar. Dom refuses the first few times. She explains that her job in international retail means she often has to participate in online meetings and conference calls during the evenings, which restricts her social life. Eventually, though, she accepts. Marco buys the most expensive bottle of champagne on the wine list. Dom knows that it is an overpriced, inferior vintage, but says nothing. She drinks up, flatters Marco's ego, hints at what Jean called "jam tomorrow," then leaves.

Marco ups the ante with flowers, gifts and fancy dinners, to no avail. Each night, as he stares at his reflection in the bathroom mirror and moisturises his skin before retiring to bed alone, he reminds himself not to feel annoyed by Dominique's behaviour. Admittedly, she is proving more of a challenge than any quarry he has ever encountered, but he tells himself that this is only to be expected from a lady of her calibre. The woman was a model, for goodness' sake, surrounded by beautiful people so, clearly, he cannot rely on his looks like he normally does. Nor can he trot out his usual lines and charm her into bed. That might have worked with Eva, but with Dominique, it is a useless tactic; she is far too sophisticated. The only answer, Marco figures, is to do something really special. He will have to deliver something that no one else can offer. Luckily, he knows just what that is.

Weeks of dancing with Dominique have shown Marco how competitive she is, so Marco is going to ensure that together, they triumph at the regional championships. He is confident that, once victory is theirs, everything else will fall into place, as it were. Indeed, he sometimes suspects that Dominique is holding out on him for this very purpose – to ensure he puts in a stellar performance on the night. If this is true, she needn't bother; he is totally committed to the contest, and this commitment would not waver, were they to indulge in some extracurricular activity beforehand. He feels like telling Dom there is no point in playing games, denying herself pleasure or postponing the inevitable, but then he checks himself. Let her play it her way. He can be patient. The waiting game will make his dual victories even sweeter.

On the night of the regional championships Jean and Eva take their places in the audience. June and Elaine are elsewhere in the auditorium, as per the cunning plan. They reserve a seat for Heather, who is looking forward to watching her wife dance, but has been held up in traffic. The two of them do not discuss what they have cooked up for Marco later on. Secrecy is essential, although they occasionally exchange a knowing smile. Eva reflects on the notion that sometimes the anticipation of pleasure is better than the reality. She hopes that this will not be true tonight.

In the dressing rooms, the tension mounts. Wardrobe and make-up malfunctions result in spectacular meltdowns, particularly among the less experienced competitors. Dominique, accustomed to the mayhem that reigns backstage during Fashion Week in London, Paris and New York, is oblivious. Not so Mrs Fry. You would think an experienced teacher like her would be inured to the chaos, but she isn't. Her hands shake as she zips Dominique into her skin-tight costume, and she twitters and fusses as Dom applies her make-up.

When she knocks over a pot of glitter-laden eyeshadow, which spews its gaudy guts across the floor, Dom's patience gives out. She desperately needs some peace and quiet in order to focus on her upcoming performance, so she cobbles together a ruse to remove her teacher from her presence, albeit temporarily.

'Mrs Fry, can you do me a favour, please?'

'Of course. What's wrong, Dominique? What do you need?'

'Nothing's wrong. I just need you to get my Latin dance shoes from Heather. She's bringing them with her. She should be arriving about now. Check with Eva and Jean – she's planning to join them.'

'What? Why has Heather got your Latin shoes? Why didn't you bring them yourself?'

'I brought my ballroom shoes by mistake, but Heather has definitely picked up my Latin shoes for me, so it's all good. I can message her if you don't want to go and find her, and ask her to come into the dressing room, but my hands are covered in glitter, and I don't want to mess up my phone – or my dress.'

'No, don't worry - I'll track her down. In the meantime, finish your face and get your hands cleaned up! I only hope Marco doesn't come up with any last-minute requests! My nerves are in shreds!'

Mrs Fry bustles off. Dom does some yogic breathing exercises, then focuses on steadying her hands, ready to apply the thick, winged eyeliner she used to wear every time she walked for Chanel. When, after fifteen minutes, her teacher still hasn't returned, Dom doesn't notice. She is absorbed in ensuring she looks perfect and outshines every other woman on the dancefloor.

Outside, in the corridor, Marco paces up and down. Dressed, made up and ready to wow the judges, he runs through every step of the rumba in his head, then visualises himself lifting the trophy as Dominique gazes up at him, her face aglow. Mrs Fry's frantic voice doesn't register; his teacher has to tug at his sleeve to get his attention.

'Marco! You've got to help me!'

'What's the matter, Mrs Fry?'

'Something terrible has happened! Heather has got Dominique's Latin shoes with her! She should have arrived by now, but I just saw Jean and Eva, who told me she's stuck in traffic, and you're due onstage for the opening parade in less than ten minutes! Dom can't go on without her shoes – it's a disaster! What are we going to do?'

Marco puts a comforting arm around Mrs Fry's shoulders.

'Don't worry. I'll sort this out, but you need to calm down and rewind. First of all, who's Heather?'

Mrs Fry looks at Marco in astonishment.

'What d'you mean, who's Heather? Heather is Dominique's wife, of course! Why else would she have Dom's shoes with her? Dom brought her ballroom shoes by mistake, so she asked Heather to bring her Latin shoes from home. I would rather she had remembered them herself, but you know Dom — she can be a bit of a princess. She's always making Heather run around after her - anyway, that's beside the point. We're wasting time — we've got to find her!'

'Heather is Dominique's wife.'

Marco repeats Mrs Fry's words in a dull monotone.

Mrs Fry doesn't answer. She doesn't even hear. Her gaze is fixed on a point beyond Marco, further down the corridor. Her face lights up. She smiles, and waves. It is almost as though she has forgotten Marco is there. Then she remembers.

'Panic over! Heather's here. I just saw her, going into the ladies dressing room with Dom's shoes. I told Jean and Eva to send her straight there if she turned up — and luckily for us, she has. Talk about cutting it fine! I'm going to need a large gin after all this is over. You dancers really do put me through the wringer. I only hope it's worth it – but I have a hunch it will be. You and Dominique are the most inspired couple I've ever coached, Marco. I've never said this before but, although the competition is fierce, I believe you two have an excellent chance of lifting the trophy tonight.'

Mrs Fry's hunch proves incorrect. Dominique and Marco are placed fourth. There is nothing technically wrong with their execution; every step is perfect, exactly as practised, but the magic is absent. Marco's performance is completely devoid of his usual passion, and Dominique responds in kind. The judges acknowledge that both are excellent dancers, but there is simply no chemistry, and if there's one thing you need to perform an outstanding rumba, it's chemistry. Most of the other couples demonstrate artistry as well as technical prowess. In the end, despite the rumours which circulated prior to the competition about the brilliant couple from Bowford Ballroom Academy, the decision is not hard to make.

Immediately after the results are announced Jean, Eva and Heather receive a WhatsApp message from Dominique:

'Cancel the plan and get me out of here.'

The women take Dominique home. She sobs and scrubs in the shower while Heather waits patiently with towels and a robe. Then, over wine, she recovers her composure and explains what happened.

'As you know, I only got my shoes just before the opening parade, so I didn't have time to speak to Marco before we went on, but I could tell something was the matter so, when the parade was over, I asked him what was wrong. He didn't answer; instead, he grabbed my arm and dragged me down the corridor and out into the car park. I'll never forget the way he looked at me, like I was a stain on one of his precious designer jackets. He accused me of deceiving him and leading him on, which I could have coped with, but the things he said about me being gay - it was just disgusting. I can't bear to repeat any of it. I thought we were done with homophobia like that in this country.'

'Sadly, we're not, babe. You're just insulated from it, in the frothy world of fashion. Out here in the real world, things are different.'

'OK, Mrs Former Police Officer. I understand what you're saying — but that doesn't mean I have to like it. That's why I'm going to call Mrs Fry tomorrow and tell her I'm leaving the academy.'

'Oh no, you're not.'

Jean's voice is firm.

'You're going to call Mrs Fry and tell her what Marco said to you. She'll ban him from dance class once she finds out what he's really like. Mrs Fry likes to win – but not that much. Not at any cost.'

'I agree with Jean. That man has caused enough pain. He has no place at Bowford Ballroom Academy. Before he arrived, it was a friendly place. It can be like that again – but only without Marco.'

'Well said, my friend.'

Jean reaches over and squeezes Eva's hand.

Eva smiles at Jean, then nods discreetly towards Heather, who has her arm around Dominique's shoulders. Heather's face is buried in Dom's beachy, brunette waves, still damp from the shower, and she is talking gently in a tone that a groom might use to comfort a highly strung thoroughbred.

'Heather - we're going to take off. Let us know if you need anything, Dom – and we'll see you in class next week. We'll show ourselves out.'

The front door closes. Heather sits up and

holds her wife at arm's length. With her thumb, she delicately wipes the mascara smudges from underneath Dom's eyes.

'Feeling any better, babe?'

'To be honest – no.'

'I see. I reckon you'd better tell me what Marco said to you, now it's just us. I know it's difficult, but I need to hear it. Every word.'

'I suppose you do. After all, it affects you as well as me.'

Heather has finally managed to schedule a drink with two of the police colleagues who were so patient with her sofa-surfing, back in the day. Although both live in Bowford, they're under-resourced and over-committed, so she hasn't seen them for months and is looking forward to necking a few pints with them. Dominique is away, so Heather knows she will neither be castigated for drunkenness nor for calorie consumption on her return home. Dom has often pointed out the supposed disconnect between Heather's love of real ale and her passion for yoga. Heather has no difficulty in reconciling the two.

Old habits die hard. Once the three of them are settled with their beer, Heather can't resist asking her friends what they're working on. Even at a time like this, when she suspects she knows the answer, she can't help herself.

Heather is partially right. DI James Radley who, predictably, goes by the nickname Boo, is still leading the investigation that officers have privately nicknamed T2. Nothing to do with the Central European Bank, nor MRI scanning, the name is short for Towpath Taser. However, DS Sandra Farrell, aka Faz, has been reassigned to a new enquiry, as T2 has hit the buffers and fewer resources are required. Of course, Heather knows none of this. She has read the press reports, but that's it. She tried to discuss the matter with Dom, but her wife told her to drop the subject. Heather doesn't blame her, but she's not here now, so she can't tell Heather to leave well alone. Heather smiles to herself. As if a former detective can be prevented from prying. Good luck with that.

A few pints in, Faz goes outside to take an urgent work call and Boo opens up.

'I suppose you want to know how that canal job is going.'

'Only if you feel like talking about it.'

'I don't mind – and there isn't much to tell, to be honest. As I'm sure you read in the local rag, we found the bloke on the towpath near the mill, and the coroner quickly confirmed heart attack as the cause of death. So far, so straightforward. Anyhow, his ex-wife was still in his phone as his emergency contact, so we paid her a visit. She wasn't particularly upset by the news.'

'They *were* divorced, Boo.'

'Yeah; and there obviously wasn't any love lost. Not on her side, at least. The funny thing was, when we broke the news of her husband's death, she didn't seem overly surprised. When I asked her why, she revealed that Marco had a congenital heart condition which could flare up anytime. Apparently the risk was set to increase as he got older. She reckons that was why he had become so selfish. Carpe diem - and sod the rest of humanity. Anyway, we contacted his doctors, and it checked out. The guy was a ticking timebomb.'

'If he died of natural causes, why are you still working on the case? Seems like a waste of your talents.'

'You're right, it would be, except we found a little something during the post-mortem that complicated matters a bit.'

'What was that?'

'Four puncture wounds. Two on his right thigh, two on his left.'

'Two pairs – so you're talking taser marks?'

'Yes – and before you ask, it wasn't one of

us. There's no instance of a taser being deployed in Bowford. We've checked with the Home Office, and they don't have a record either. As you know, we have to inform them every time we so much as remove a taser from its holster. Also, it appears the attackers were aiming for the crown jewels. Not an approach that is sanctioned by us rozzers.'

'What's your hypothesis, Boo?'

'No, Heather – you first. Let me enjoy my beer while you tell me what you think happened.'

'It's not so much about what happened, in my opinion. It's more to do with the motive and the intention behind the assault. What happened is that one, or possibly two assailants tasered the victim, triggering a fatal heart attack. The question is – were they aware that this Marco guy had a cardiac condition? Did they mean to kill him, or just cause a temporary, albeit painful shock?'

'Exactly. That's what we're trying to establish.'

'Also, how did they manage to procure a taser?'

'You have heard of the dark web, Heather? It's an offshoot of this little thing called the internet.'

'Very funny. And then there's the small

matter of who would want to harm or kill Marco. Did the guy have any enemies?'

'How long have you got, Heather? Where do I start? Maybe with his landlord. Apparently Marco was months behind with the rent on his swanky penthouse apartment. Poor bloke was desperate to evict him and replace him with a tenant who would actually pay up. Then you have the neighbours. Turns out Marco was locked in disputes with several of them about noise, parking spaces – you name it. Next we come on to his career. Suffice to say that Marco was not Mr Popular in the workplace. All style and no substance, apparently. Sucked up to the bosses, got everyone else to do the heavy lifting, then claimed all the credit. You know the type. Some of his colleagues reckon he lied on his CV. Talked his way into a senior position, then couldn't hack it. Also, he slept his way around the office. Seems he could charm his way into any woman's bed, including the chief exec's PA, who was married at the time. Her ex-husband would be top of our long list of suspects if he didn't have a cast-iron alibi. You get the picture?'

'What about Marco's ex? Does she have an alibi too?'

'Indeed, she does. It checks out perfectly.

However, as I think we've established, there are plenty of other candidates with good reason to wish the victim harm. In fact, the only people who rate Marco are the dancers – and the teacher - at the academy attended by your wife. I suppose it's easier to remain charmed by someone if you don't live, work or sleep with them.'

'I guess so. You've interviewed most of the dancers, I take it? And Mrs Fry, the teacher?'

'Absolutely – and they were all in agreement. Marco was the best thing to happen to the dance academy for years. He made them all raise their game, and they were excited to watch him perform with Dominique at the regional championships. Obviously they were disappointed he didn't win, but it was still a good result for the academy. The dance teacher couldn't work out what had gone wrong, but when she heard about his heart condition, she said that explained everything. Apparently Marco had seemed unwell on the night of the championships, right before his performance. All flushed and tense. She had put it down to nerves, but now she realised his heart problem was to blame. Why else would he deliver such a mediocre performance when he was expected to win?'

'Why indeed? Dom couldn't figure it out. She was gutted. My wife isn't a fourth-place kind of person, but I helped her move on. Let's rewind, though. You said that it's "easier to remain charmed by someone if you don't live, work or sleep with them." Why didn't Marco sleep with any of the dancers, Boo? Why didn't he work his way through them, like he did his co-workers? I mean, there are some attractive women in the academy. There's Eva, for a start, and her dance partner Elaine is lovely too. She's married, but by all accounts, that wouldn't deter Marco. There are quite a few others whom no self-respecting man would kick out of bed – so what was holding Marco back? Why didn't he fill his boots?'

'Oh, Heather. You're too close to this, love. I asked the dancers the same question, and they each gave the same answer. It was because of Dom.'

'What?'

'He was obsessed with your wife, and we both know why. The woman has star quality. She's in a different league from the others. How you pulled her is anyone's guess.'

'Cheers for that, Boo. But why would Marco waste his time on a gay woman?'

'There's a simple answer. He didn't know

she was gay. It didn't even occur to him.'

'Didn't anyone think to tell him?'

'A few of them did. They felt bad about him wasting his time like that, but they collectively decided to keep quiet until after the dance competition, so they wouldn't upset him and potentially ruin his chances – and Dom's.'

'I see. Dom never mentioned it to me.'

'Why would she? Your wife must have to fend people off with a sharp stick, the whole time. She probably didn't think it was worth mentioning.'

'Fair point.'

'Also, you said yourself how much she likes to win. I guess she thought she could channel his ardour to her advantage, as it were.'

'You could be right. I'm going to FaceTime her later – I'll ask her then.'

'We'll need to have a chat with her when she returns from Brazil. Just for completeness – so we've interviewed everyone from the dance academy.'

'You could do an online interview if you like. She wouldn't mind.'

'No, it's fine. She was away when the attack took place, so she's low on our priority list.'

'Hopefully she'll be back soon. I didn't expect her to have to go back out there at short notice. That team in Rio couldn't organise a piss-up in a brewery.'

'Talking of which, we're out of beer, and here comes Faz. By the look of her, she needs another pint.'

'I'll go, Boo. It's my round. Thanks for the update on the investigation. It's good to know that the ladies at the academy aren't caught up in it. Dom's become quite fond of them.'

'My money's on one of Marco's noisy neighbours. The bloke's got form – he was charged with GBH as a youngster but got off on a technicality. A few years later, he was convicted of possession with intent to supply. He's a bad lad, and so are his mates. I reckon he tasered old Marco to teach him a lesson for complaining about the racket and got more than he bargained for. I'm focusing my attention on him – not on a bunch of mild-mannered ballroom dancers in cardigans.'

'Sounds very sensible. Same again?'

'Please, Heather.'

At the bar, Heather orders three pints of local bitter and a large whisky chaser. She glances across the room to where Boo and Faz are deep in conversation, their heads bent close together. Heather turns away from them, necks the whisky in one gulp, then pulls her phone from her pocket. A quick social media search reveals that the local rugby team is ahead at half time. The three friends are rugby fans; her update on the score is bound to generate a lively discussion. It will be a relief to steer the conversation away from police matters after her informative but stressful dialogue with Boo. She picks up the beer glasses and makes her way back to the table.

The Indian summer finally arrives in Bowford. It's a little late this year, but Jean and June never doubted it would come. June arranges two sun loungers on either side of a small round table in her back garden, then lifts the cumbersome parasol with difficulty. On her second wobbly attempt, she slots it into the hole in the centre of the table, then opens it. She returns to the kitchen, cursing her husband, who was supposed to have put the garden furniture out for them before he went to the pub.

June carries a plate of mini rolls out to the garden and places it carefully on the table. She angles the parasol so as to shade the mini rolls from the sun and prevent them from melting, then heads back to the kitchen and opens the fridge. The doorbell rings twice in quick succession, but she makes no move to answer it. Two rings means that Jean is here, and her friend knows to let herself in.

Jean carries the flutes and June follows her with the Prosecco. They settle themselves on the sun loungers and hoick up their skirts, remarking that it's nice to get some sun to their legs. June pops the cork on the fizz and charges their glasses. Jean gulps half of hers and unwraps a mini roll, whilst grumbling about the half stone she has regained. She puts it down to the stress she has been under in recent weeks. Her friend smiles and pats her bare knee.

'You can relax now, Jean.'

'I know, but I reckon it'll take a while to sink in, to be honest. Who would have guessed that Marco's neighbour would turn out to be even more dodgy than the man himself?'

'Did you read the piece in the local paper, about the guy being done for drugs?'

'Yes - and grievous bodily harm.'

'He got off that, though.'

'On a technicality, whatever that's supposed to mean, but it's obvious he did it. What a nasty piece of work. Good job he's off the streets. I'm surprised the police didn't arrest him sooner.'

'Maybe they would have done, except they

had to eliminate everyone else from the enquiry. Marco's ex-wife, his colleagues, his other neighbours – not to mention all of us.'

'You're right. It's not like on the TV, where the cops can just back their hunches, swoop in and arrest the culprit. They have to plough through a load of pointless interviews with other people first.'

'At least we helped them out. We made sure everyone at the academy was singing from the same hymn sheet – or should I say, dancing to the same tune.'

'Very funny. You're right though, June – we did well. We saved the police from wasting time investigating minor inconsistencies. Without us, they'd have headed off down all sorts of rabbit holes. It's a shame they'll never know how much they owe us.'

'Best they don't, Jean.'

'I suppose not.'

'I'm glad you agree. Drink up.'

June refills their glasses. The bottle is emptying fast, but she has another in the fridge. They rarely have a two-bottle session, but today she has decided to make an exception.

'So, are you OK, Jean?'

'Why wouldn't I be? I've got sunshine, chocolate, Prosecco, and my best mate by my side. What's not to love?'

'Don't be flippant. You know what I mean.'

'Any regrets? Is that what you're trying to say?'

'That's right. Given that we over-achieved, as Eva put it.'

'I know, but I don't feel guilty. I've only got one regret, truth be told.'

'What's that, Jean?'

'I'm sorry I missed.'

'Really?'

'Really. Turns out Mrs Fry was right all along. Hand-eye co-ordination doesn't come naturally to me.'

'I wouldn't worry. Eva and I were on target. Well, almost.'

'Close enough, my friend. Close enough.'

16 THE LEVEL CROSSING

The wide Fenland skies pulsed with angry storm clouds blowing in from the west. The endless fields, their crops swaying in mass submission to the strengthening wind, were bisected only by the railway line and the road, which ran parallel for miles, then converged, right in front of William's modest, rather forlorn house. Standing alone in the vast landscape, with only a few shabby outbuildings and the level crossing for company, it was exactly the sort of house a child would draw.

William stood at his bedroom window, contemplating the view upon which he had gazed for fifty years. The gates of the level crossing opposite his front door were shut tight like clenched teeth. No cars queued to cross the tracks; only a lone cyclist waited patiently on a rusty shopper bike so different from the flashy models ridden by the Lycra warriors who passed this way on weekends. Her narrow back and straight dark hair, gathered in a ponytail at the nape of her neck, gave her a fragile look. As William watched, she dismounted, leant her bike against the gates, then seized them, trying to pull them apart. William thought her unlikely to succeed.

The scene transported William back to a summer's day, almost thirty years previously, when another young cyclist, impatient to continue his journey, had forced open the gates so he could cross the apparently deserted railway line. Watching from his kitchen window and with the timetable etched in his memory, William knew that the express train was just moments away. As the boy wedged his bike through the gap in the gates and wriggled after it, William raced across the road and pulled the boy back from the brink, seconds before the train thundered past, having appeared seemingly from nowhere. Shamefaced and tearful, the boy waited in the hallway afterwards while William called his parents and arranged for them to pick him up.

Only recently, William had read in the

paper that this same boy, now managing director of a local packaging company, had automated his factory and made nearly half the workforce redundant. The article criticised him for retaining his six-figure salary and lavish lifestyle whilst putting people out of work. William wondered whether he had done the right thing in rescuing him.

William watched the girl's futile struggle with the gates until, without warning, she abandoned her efforts, stood back, then vaulted over with easy grace, leaving her bike behind. The express train was due imminently. Finding a turn of speed that he had not thought possible at his age, William rushed downstairs and hurled himself across the road, leaving his front door swinging wildly in the wind.

The girl spotted him and immediately dropped to her knees. In a gesture which seemed incredibly poignant to William, she carefully removed her wire-framed spectacles and placed them on the ground, then crawled forward and laid her slender frame across the track. William barely had time to seize her windcheater and pull her clear before the express roared past. The backdraft knocked them off their feet as the girl screamed at the top of her lungs, angry at having been rescued.

Unrepentant, William gently guided the girl back to his house. Over several pots of tea, he listened while she explained, sobbing, that she had been bullied for years at school, her only friend had abandoned her and she had discovered her boyfriend was only dating her for a dare, to amuse the bullies. Her dad left when she was a baby and her mum struggled with drink and drugs. Her name was Lucy and she had no one to turn to. No hope.

William gently disagreed, explaining how he, too, had been an outcast whose teenage years were a misery but had found love in this lonely place and treasured it for ever. He recounted how, although his beloved wife was dead, he still felt her presence every day, in the birds' bleak cries and the clouds rolling through the immensity of the Fenland sky.

Afterwards, Lucy often came for tea with William on her battered shopper bike. She liked her new school, organised by her mum once she found the courage to explain to her. She enjoyed catering college even more and often tested her baking recipes on William. When he had a stroke, some years later, Lucy visited him in hospital and taught him how to hold a teacup again. Then, when William finally left his lonely house behind and moved into a care home, Lucy and her children brought him cakes every week and her husband smuggled in some illicit homebrew. Eventually, when it was time for William to go, Lucy's smiling face was the last one he saw, as he squeezed her hand, smiled back and finally closed his eyes.

17 DILLON'S DAY OUT

Detective Sergeant Kevin Wright switched off the projector and grimly surveyed his operational unit. It was time to crank up the pre-dawn energy levels. The team's bleary eyes were understandable, but not acceptable. On a job like this, total focus was imperative. He dropped his heavy folder onto the table with a crash. The officers sat up hastily.

'Before we deploy, I want to say one last thing. Our target is a highly dangerous criminal. For years he has brought misery and death to our streets. We have failed to apprehend him several times, but today, thanks to reliable intelligence, we have our best ever chance of nailing him. However, we'll only succeed if each one of you gives it one hundred and ten percent. For the next few hours, nothing else matters. Our villain will do anything to evade capture, but I'm confident you're better than he is. Prove me right.'

As the team filed out of the briefing room, Kevin intercepted Detective Constable Tom Ridley, a recent transferee from Greater Manchester Police, who was far too cocky for his liking.

'You clear about what you need to do, Tom?'

'Of course, Sarge. We ran these operations every day at GMP. I know how to work the Big Red Key. It's not rocket science.'

'Fair enough, but I need to warn you about something.'

'What's that?'

'PD Dillon.'

'A *police dog*?'

Kevin smiled at Tom's incredulity.

'As it says in the advertisements, this is no ordinary police dog. Ever watched Game of Thrones?'

'Sure. My wife and I love that show.'

'Seen those huge, snarling direwolves, with their massive fangs?'

'I have.'

'They're toy poodles, compared with

Dillon. If that dog is off the lead, do *not* get out of your car. Not if you want to finish this operation with all your limbs intact.'

'Are you being serious, Sarge?'

'Deadly. That dog's a legend around here, but not always in a good way. He's very effective, but he doesn't discriminate between criminals and police officers. You have been warned.'

The dark Fenland horizon was backlit by the neon glow of the oncoming dawn. As vivid pink streaks lightened the sky, a solitary drone picked out, far below, a convoy of toy cars gliding down a long, straight road, elevated above the treacle-black soil of the endless fields. A lone farmhouse stood sentinel over the bleak landscape. The convoy halted well clear of the house, whilst the drone shifted position and hovered over the scene, waiting.

Figures emerged silently from the vehicles and walked in. Some formed a cordon around the farmhouse, whilst the remainder gathered at the front door, where DC Ridley wrestled his unwieldy burden into position. Nearby a small dog looked on, wagging its tail excitedly. Then DS Wright whispered a single word:

'Go!'

Instantly the place erupted. With a single

burst of kinetic energy, DC Ridley swung his battering ram backwards, then let the forward momentum of the Big Red Key do its job on the front door. The hinges exploded upon impact, the wood splintered into a pile of useless shards and the officers leapt over them, shouting wildly. Meanwhile the small dog, tail still wagging, eagerly began executing the task for which it had been trained.

In the back bedroom, an officer clasped cold handcuffs around the sleep-warm wrists of an outraged, struggling woman. Through the window, he spotted a lone figure running away across the fields, then smiled to himself as a massive white maelstrom of fur, teeth and claws gave chase. High above, the drone captured the relentless trajectory of PD Dillon as he rapidly closed in on his quarry, took off from yards away, locked his jaws onto the man's arm and used his combined weight and speed to bring him down. His target fought back aggressively, trying to plunge the fingers of his free hand into the dog's eyes, but it was no use. By the time Dillon's breathless handler arrived on the scene, the drug dealer was subdued and compliant.

Meanwhile, back in the house, PD Maisie stood, motionless, beside the largest ever drugs haul in the county. She was trained to highlight the presence of narcotics by not moving a muscle, so her wagging tail was temporarily stilled, until her handler presented her with a tennis ball, the ultimate reward for a happy spaniel who embodied the phrase: 'work hard, play hard.'

That evening, PD Dillon lay sprawled on the sofa next to his handler, Police Constable Rick Marshall, who tickled him affectionately behind the ears.

'It's a good job Mummy's out tonight, Dillon, or you'd never get away with this. Still, you caught a bad man today, so I reckon you deserve it. Beer?'

Dillon slowly lifted his huge head, one side of which was still streaked with dried blood where the drug dealer had gone for his eyes. He pricked up his ears and his tail thumped rhythmically against the sofa cushions.

'Thought so. Here you go.'

Rick guided his pint glass towards Dillon's muzzle. Eagerly the dog pushed his snout inside and lapped the dregs of Rick's beer. When he had finished, he withdrew his glistening wet nose and looked expectantly at his handler.

'You know what comes next, don't you, boy?'

Rick shoved his fist inside a crackling plastic bag and withdrew what looked like a gnarled, discoloured toenail.

'Time for a nice pork scratching.'

Dillon's huge jaws made short work of the pub snack. Afterwards, he flopped down on Rick's lap with a contented sigh.

'This is our secret, right? We can't have the criminal fraternity finding out you're a lapdog. You must continue putting them behind bars, and you can only do that if they're scared of you. So, let's keep it to ourselves.'

Lost in his doggy dream world, the legend that was PD Dillon responded with a slight twitch of the leg.

Author's Note

This story is a work of fiction, as are the characters.

All except PD Dillon. Sadly, he's no longer with us, but while he lived, he was a legend who terrorised police officers and criminals alike.

18 TRICK OR TREAT?

As Emily finished cooking, the sun surrendered to night.

The food tasted bland, but he had been adamant. No garlic.

She put on his gift - a low-cut dress that showed off her slender neck, with its creamy skin.

The sky turned black.

Then came the knock at the door.

19 LIFE CYCLE

This is my favourite part. I love being up in the sky, locked in a fluffy white cloud along with millions just like me. Mind you, the clouds only appear fluffy to onlookers like you. In here, it's hazy and formless.

Soon, as always, everything changes. Milky white darkens to slate grey, then to black. I grow heavier and am drawn inexorably towards the earth. I condense, then go into free-fall. The shrieking wind ruins my downward trajectory, flinging me sideways onto a tiled roof. I fall with a painless splat, quickly regain my shape and roll downhill into a gutter.

There are lots of us in here. We cling together and others join in. At first we're just a tiny trickle, then gradually we gain critical mass, forming a crystal stream that cascades along the gutter and plunges into the darkness of a vertical pipe. We tumble downwards, then abruptly change course and are thrust, horizontally and headlong, towards our destination.

When we emerge into the daylight, we join billions of others. Together we create a majestic expanse of blue, fringed by feathery trees. Ducks and geese float on our surface. Below, fish breathe us in. Sadly, I have little time to savour the experience. All too soon I'm dragged downwards on another dark odyssey through a network of pipes.

In the next place, the smell tells me where I am. Once I formed part of a swimming pool which smelt similar. I've been here many times before. This is where I get spruced up. When they're done with me, I'll be clean, clear and, most importantly, safe. I wriggle through layers of sand that are coarse at first, then fine and densely packed. Gradually I leave my impurities behind among the golden grains. Finally, I receive a nip of the swimming pool stuff - just to make sure – then the process is complete. I feel light, free and fit for purpose. I'm ready to fulfil my destiny.

Soon afterwards, I gush from a metal

spigot into a clear container. I peer through it and see a clean room, with sparkling tiles and gleaming chrome. Abruptly the view is obscured by pink fingers which grasp the vessel and tilt it. Down I slide, into a new world of soft, pulsating red. It's warm in here and the pipes are narrow and yielding. For a change, they're made of flesh, not plastic. On this part of my voyage, I hydrate my host. I cleanse. I maintain life. I scoop up harmful particles and change colour along the way. When I take my leave, my host is a little healthier and no longer thirsty. I've done my job, this time round, but my journey is far from over.

This part is not as bad as you might imagine. Sure, I have a few malodorous companions, but they get diluted and dissolved by millions of my colleagues who have been discharged from washing machines, baths and sinks. We swirl together in an opaque, beige torrent, cascading through the darkness until we're ejected into what can only be described as a feeding frenzy.

Under a leaden sky, we get sprayed onto rocks which are coated with ravenous bacteria. These insatiable microbes feast upon our impurities, rendering us fit to join the river nearby. As I thank them and take my leave, I'm aware that I'm not in the pristine condition I was earlier. I won't be that clean again. Not this time round. Ah, well – at least I won't poison the fish.

I enjoy being part of the river. I babble over gravel, idle in deep, slow-moving pools and let centrifugal force whirl me around the outside of the bends. I drift past a heron who snatches a wriggling, silver fish. I flow underneath moorhen chicks which bob on the surface like miniature powder puffs, and I pray they won't be spotted by the lurking, low-lying pike. Then I emerge into the vast expanse of the estuary.

The sun has come out. It beats down without remorse upon the surface. I bask in the heat. It feels like a long time since I was this warm. Then it starts to happen. Gradually, I feel myself getting lighter and lighter, until I rediscover the joy of weightlessness. I break free from the sea and am drawn upwards into the blue. Others like me are compelled to join in, and soon we band together. In the expanse of clear sky, we form a single, fluffy white cloud.

20 SEA CHANGE

'Travel broadens the mind.'

Martin deployed this well-worn cliché to talk his wife Sophie into taking a holiday on the Costa del Sol. The odd thing was, it worked, although not immediately. Sophie was not the impulsive type.

Reflecting on the two years since her retirement, Sophie realised she had pursued two goals – broad mind, narrow body – and achieved more success with the former than with the latter. Voracious reading, theatre and gallery trips with like-minded friends, and volunteer work at her local food bank had revived a brain dulled by decades of monotonous office work in local government. However, despite regular gym workouts, cycle rides and Pilates classes, her body stubbornly remained the same width, and her stomach was not as toned as she would have liked. Sophie told herself that rock-hard abs were an unrealistic goal at her age. Nevertheless, she felt disappointed as she contemplated the modest layer of squodge that no amount of stomach crunching would shift. Then she lowered her gaze and cheered up. Her legs were still OK. She remembered reading in a beauty magazine that one's legs were the last to go.

Then Sophie thought about the Costa del Sol. Despite Martin's assertion, she doubted that the place would broaden her mind any further. She imagined Carling lager, football shirts and liberally tattooed bodies. Irish bars. Serried ranks of sun loungers topped with tourists whose oiled, sunburned bodies glistened like the Christmas ham she carefully basted each year. Then her inner voice, always her worst critic, forced a rethink.

'Call yourself broad-minded? You're nothing of the kind. You're just a snob!'

Sophie went through to the sitting room, where Martin was watching the golf.

'I've thought it through, darling – and I've decided I'd like to go to the Costa del Sol. I could do with some sun.'

'Great. As soon as the golf's finished, I'll get it booked.'

Sophie was right. Her preconceptions had been way off. The Irish bars were confined to the town centre a mile away and the elegant bar in their hotel lobby served Sangria, cocktails, and local beer. Not a pint of Carling nor a football shirt in sight.

On the first morning, she decided to hit the hotel gym. Martin watched sleepily from their bed as she got changed.

'I'm not being funny, love, but you might want to rethink the crop top. I'm not saying you don't look good. It's just that...'

'At my age?'

'Exactly.'

'Point taken.'

Sophie covered the offending garment with a baggy T-shirt she had planned to use for her cooldown.

'Better?'

'Much. Look, I'm going to treat myself to a lie-in. If I'm not here when you get back, I'll be having breakfast at the beach bar. Come and join me.'

Sophie regarded her husband as he lay sprawled across the bed. He was still so handsome, after all these years. Not drop-dead, boy-band handsome, like when they first met, but distinguished older-man handsome, with tastefully greying hair and ice-blue eyes. His olive skin was only slightly mottled, and he sported less midriff podge than Sophie, despite his lifelong aversion to exercise. There was no justice, Sophie concluded.

'OK, Martin. See you later.'

The air conditioning in the gym was broken. After five minutes on the treadmill, Sophie whipped off her T-shirt. Martin would never know. She worked out for forty minutes, then gave up and dripped her way to the towel station next to the gym reception desk, her hair plastered to her skull. Rivulets of sweat trickled down her forehead and into her eyes, stinging and blurring her vision. As she searched in vain for a towel, she heard footsteps behind her, followed by a deep sigh.

'What a surprise. No towels...as per usual. Manolo!'

The door marked 'Privada' opened, and a harassed looking man appeared.

'Hola, Señor Caballo!'

The customer replied with a volley of rapid-fire Spanish, then turned to Sophie.

'Towels are on their way.'

'Thank you, Señor...'

'Alan. You can call me Al.'

'I'm Sophie. Bet you never cracked that joke before.'

'Busted. Only other Brits get it, though, and I don't speak to many of them, these days.'

'How come? Are you a hermit?'

'Sort of. I live up in the hills. I only venture down here for the gym and the market.'

'Hence your fluent Spanish.'

'Not fluent, but close enough. You have to learn fast if you marry a native and end up running an animal sanctuary by mistake. That's why Manolo has nicknamed me Señor Caballo. Mr Horse.'

'I see. Sounds intriguing.'

'Exhausting, more like. Come and visit. Bring your...husband?'

Alan rummaged in his gym bag and produced a crumpled business card.

'Husband. Yes. Martin. Er...look, Al. Here are the towels.'

'Muchas gracias, Manolo.'

Alan peeled off his sodden T-shirt and mopped his chest, arms, and sun-bleached hair without a trace of self-consciousness. Sophie looked away, buried her face in her own towel and tried to decide how to respond to his invitation. Their conversation had flowed so easily, but now she felt awkward. Suddenly she was conscious of her puce face and soaking wet crop top. She wrapped her towel around her body, desperate to escape.

'We're only here for a fortnight, so I'm not sure we'll have time. Maybe we will...we'll see.'

'Sure. No pressure. Enjoy your holiday, Sophie.'

Martin quickly acquired a group of cronies, along with a deep tan, despite rarely venturing out from under the beach bar veranda. Meanwhile Sophie slathered herself with sun cream and morphed from bluish white to pale gold. She braved the freezing sea, shivered through aqua aerobics in the pool, powered through numerous books on her Kindle and worked out daily. The gym was usually empty, and she never saw Alan again. Each evening she joined her husband for dinner and drinks. The bars stayed open late, and after the first couple of days she took to retiring before they closed, leaving Martin to shoot the breeze with his newfound friends. She was usually asleep when he returned to their room. Every morning he slept later, until one morning, he didn't surface at all.

'Sorry, Soph – I don't feel great today.

Touch of man 'flu. Can you manage on your own?'

'Sure. I think I'll wander into town.'

'OK. Take care, love. See you this evening. Reckon I'll feel better by then.'

Sophie knew he would. Martin's hangovers always evaporated come Happy Hour.

It was market day in town. Sophie tried not to look like a tourist, failed miserably and was talked into buying a beaded ankle bracelet she knew she would never wear at home. As she bent down to slip it over her foot, she heard a familiar voice behind her, speaking to the stallholder. When she stood up, the stallholder handed her a matching necklace.

'No, sorry...I just want the bracelet. Er...solo el...'

The stallholder shrugged in response.

'Relax.'

Alan smiled at her.

'I asked him to throw it in for free.'

'I don't want him to lose money...'

'He won't. Trust me. His margins are huge.'

'In that case – thanks.'

'You never came – to see me and my animals.'

'Sorry. My husband's not one for day trips.'

'Not even to the market, I see.'

'No. Particularly not today. He's ill.'

'So, why don't you come now? I've just got to pick up some overripe fruit and veg that the market traders can't sell. They give them to me free.'

'Can you drive me back by four? I'll be missed if I'm any later.'

'Absolutely. Scout's honour.'

The battered van snaked its way uphill. Below, the sea stretched out misty blue. Alan pointed out the purple outline of the Atlas mountains on the far side. Sophie was enchanted to see another continent, far away on the horizon. Once she was done staring, she turned her gaze from Africa back to Europe, where cacti burst triumphantly from the parched earth at the roadside. Olive trees clothed the hills in orderly lines, reminding Sophie of the ill-advised cornrows sported by some of her fellow guests.

Suddenly the van turned sharp left, revealing a rocky valley dominated by a sprawling whitewashed house surrounded by cypress trees, wooden stables and dusty paddocks. As they headed downhill, Sophie spotted horses, donkeys, pigs, and a pair of alpacas.

Alan parked up in the yard and Sophie stepped from the van. An ancient, portly dog struggled to his feet and waddled towards her on unsteady legs. Sophie bent and scratched him behind the ears.

'That's Miguel. He doesn't normally bother to greet strangers. You're honoured.'

A tall, slim brunette in jodhpurs and a white shirt emerged from one of the stables and shouted at Alan in Spanish.

'Your wife?'

Alan shouted back. The woman gave a thumbs up and disappeared.

'No. That's Alicia, my head groom. My wife jumped ship years ago.'

'I'm sorry.'

'Don't be. She was from northern Spain. Culturally, I think she was further from home than me. Initially she was OK living here, but eventually it got too much. She went to walk the Camino De Santiago with a friend from home, and never came back. It was the right decision – for both of us. I loved her, but she wasn't my soulmate.'

'Don't tell me you believe in The One.'

'I do. Buddhists say that when you meet your soulmate, your heart doesn't race. You don't go weak at the knees. You just feel calm.'

Alan paused for a moment and stared up at the cypress trees. Then he walked round to the back of the van and opened the doors.

'Fancy helping me feed the animals?'

'I'd love to.'

Sophie was charmed by the pigs and amused by the alpacas' demented expressions. She petted the donkeys and stroked the velvet noses of the horses.

'Don't you think horses have the most beautiful eyes? Like shiny melted chocolate.'

'Apart from Freda. Come and meet her.'

Alan led Sophie to a loosebox in a shady corner of the yard.

'Freda's eyes don't shine, and she likes her own company. You'll see why.'

Freda's gaze was milky white and sightless. Sophie silently reached out her hand, stopping inches short of the old girl's muzzle. After a long moment, the mare stepped forward and pushed her nose into Sophie's palm.

'Wow. She doesn't normally respond like that, but I somehow knew she'd like you.'

At that moment, a bell resounded across the yard.

'Perfect timing – not. I've got to go, I'm afraid. Visitor alert.'

'I can help with your visitors.'

'Are you sure?'

'Absolutely.'

The visitors were a family from Birmingham. Sophie and the children played with the animals, while Alan told the parents how he had renovated the derelict ranch with the money he had saved from decades spent teaching English in Malaga. It had been intended purely as a home, but the locals, hearing about his empty stables and paddocks, had begun rocking up with stray, sick and unwanted animals. Before long, he had an expensive sanctuary on his hands and relied heavily on donations in order to care for more seriously afflicted animals who couldn't be rehomed. The family stayed for two hours and donated generously as they left. Alan was delighted.

'You're my lucky charm, Sophie. No-one has stumped up that much cash in forever.'

'Glad I could help.'

'So, are you happy?'

'Odd question, but yes. I've had a lovely day.'

'I mean – in general. With life.'

'That's a bit personal, isn't it?'

'Forgive me, but I left England long ago. I've dispensed with the social niceties of Blighty. Sophie, I suspect you're not happy. With your life. With your husband.'

So, there it was. Sophie had a choice. She

could feign outrage or answer honestly. She decided on the latter.

'You're wrong. I have a perfectly nice life, with lots of friends and hobbies. As for my husband, we rub along just fine. We each do our own thing. We never row. All good.'

'I thought not.'

'What d'you mean?'

'You know what I mean. Sophie, I'll only ask once. Stay. I know you felt it too – when we first met. The peaceful feeling, like the Buddhists say. Don't go back to England. Stay here with me.'

Sophie heard her sharp tone from a distance, as if someone else was speaking.

'Don't be ridiculous. I've had a wonderful time, but now I'd be grateful if you'd drive me back.'

'As you wish.'

Sophie steeled herself for an awkward journey in stony silence, but Alan surprised her. As the van laboured its way back up the narrow track towards the main road, he said gently:

'Obviously I feel you've made the wrong call, but I respect your decision. Now, we only have a few precious moments left together. Precious to me, at least. Let's talk about something else.'

Soon the van pulled up outside the hotel. Alan reached over and kissed Sophie on both cheeks.

'Adiós, beautiful lady. I'm glad I met you.'

'Me too. I'm sorry, Al. I didn't mean to sound harsh, or rude.'

'Don't be sorry. It's fine. Safe journey home.'

Sophie scuttled into the hotel without looking back. As she walked along the corridor to their room, her eyes smarted with unshed tears. She blinked rapidly, wiped them, then forced a smile as she opened the door.

'Hello, darling. Feeling better?'

'Yes, thanks. Woah – what's that smell? Not being funny, but you reek of horse manure.'

'I visited a petting zoo. That must be it.'

'You'd better jump in the shower. You don't want to miss Happy Hour on our last night.'

Next morning, Martin slept through the journey to the airport, while Sophie checked her diary for the following week. There was plenty to keep her occupied. Soon, she realised, Spain would seem like an evanescent dream.

There was a long queue at check-in. After an eternity, Sophie lugged her suitcase onto the weighing machine. The man at the desk attached a tag and pressed a button. Her case lurched away after Martin's, into the unknown. Sophie watched it disappear, then followed her husband towards Security.

Martin passed through the barrier first. Sophie was right behind him. She opened her passport and placed it on the scanner. Immediately her heart began to pound, and she felt nauseous. She realised she was the opposite of peaceful. The Buddhists would not approve. She called anxiously to her husband:

'Martin! I need the loo!'

Her husband scowled, embarrassed. He hated it when Sophie made a show in public.

'Come through! There'll be one after Security!'

'I can't wait that long! The queues are bound to be massive. I'll catch you up.'

Martin shrugged and turned away, eager to get on. Sophie waited until he was out of sight, then looked for the sign. There it was. Funny how the word was the same in almost every language.

Taxi.

Sophie shoved her passport in her handbag and walked towards the exit. The automatic doors opened, then closed behind her.

21 DAILY GRIND

Like yours, my world is round. I circumnavigate it with ease.

Keep me company?

Here's the plant, whose leaves sway incessantly.

Here's the treasure chest, whose lid opens and closes with monotonous regularity.

Here's the log, prostrate on the gravel.

Here's the plant again.

It's dead boring, being a goldfish.

22 ICE MAGIC

Wearily she surveyed the photo. No-one in the bar matched up although, based on past experience, she was looking for someone ten years older, and two stone heavier than the man in the picture. Nervously she ruffled her sleek blonde bob, wondering why she had wasted a haircut on this guy and bothered to jazz up her jeans with a sequinned top.

Suddenly, someone tapped her on the shoulder, and she jumped.

'Hi – Natalie? I'm Ben. Sorry - I've broken Online Dating Rule Number One by being late. Are you OK? You look shocked.'

'Hi, Ben. I'm OK - just surprised. You look exactly like your photo. That's rare.'

With his mid-brown hair and unremarkable

features, Ben would never get picked out in a police identity parade.

'There's no point in faking or filtering, I think. Better to under-promise and over-deliver…oh God, sorry – I didn't mean…'

'No worries,' interrupted Natalie, taking pity on him. 'Let's get a drink.'

To break the ice, they broke Online Dating Rule Number Two – don't discuss your exes.

'Well, you win the drama prize!' Ben conceded. 'I never met someone whose husband left her for her cousin. I must seem boring, just drifting apart from my ex. If you can bear to spend more time with someone so dull, let's have dinner next week. I know a lovely Vietnamese restaurant.'

Natalie hesitated.

'OK. That would be nice.'

On the way home, she chastised herself for agreeing to a second date and worried what Ruth would say.

'So, let's get this straight.'

Ruth grabbed the wine bottle and refilled their glasses.

'There was no spark – no chemistry between you and this guy. Yet you accepted a second date – why?'

'I suppose I wimped out.'

Natalie hung her head.

'He just seemed like a nice person. I didn't want to hurt his feelings.'

'Nat. If you are going to meet Mr Right, you haven't got time for "nice." Bin him! Move on.'

'I'll give him one more chance. If dinner doesn't work out, I'll say goodbye.'

Ruth put her head in her hands.

The restaurant was intimate; unlike the conversation, which flowed as freely as the sticky rice balanced on their chopsticks. Politely they discussed their jobs. Ben's stilted account of life as an auditor failed to break down the barriers, so Natalie ploughed gamely on, describing the record company where she worked. Although her procurement role was unglamorous, her anecdotes about dissolute, stroppy musicians usually made people laugh – but tonight they fell flat. Desperately she changed the subject to hobbies. They had more success there as they both loved outdoor pursuits, particularly skiing.

Suddenly, Ben began twisting his napkin nervously and Natalie sensed that he was working up to something. She was right.

'Um - a group of us are going skiing. One person has dropped out and I thought you might like to come. You'd have your own room, and the snow conditions are excellent – loads of powder. I'm just asking you as a friend. No pressure or anything…'

Ben tailed off and fiddled with his chopsticks as he waited for an answer.

Natalie hesitated, thought of Ruth's predictable response, then decided to defy her judgmental best friend.

'What the hell,' she concluded. 'I deserve some fun.'

'Well, if you're promising powder, I'm in,' she replied. 'I love powder. I just hate ice.'

'You've got to be joking.'

Ruth peered censoriously over her glasses at Natalie.

'You can't even converse, yet you're going skiing? I give up. Here's my final piece of advice for you to ignore - bag yourself a ski instructor. Hopefully you'll have a few hotties to choose from.'

The ski trip was surprisingly successful. Everyone was single except Karen and Isobel and the group bonded well over numerous après-ski beers. As promised, the snow was superb. Natalie and Karen, both intermediates, skied together every day, whilst

Ben tackled the most challenging black runs early on, then spent the afternoons helping Isobel, who was a novice and in ski school every morning.

On the last afternoon, Karen and Natalie sat together in a bar overlooking the nursery slopes. Karen had twisted her knee earlier and was planning to miss the next morning's skiing, which the others were fitting in before their flight home.

'Look at Ben – he is so patient. Izzy says she learns more from him than from her ski instructor, as he is so kind and explains everything really well.'

Karen smiled affectionately as Isobel toppled over once again.

'You're right,' agreed Natalie. 'It's rare to find an expert skier who is prepared to help a beginner. Fancy another vin chaud?'

The following morning, Ben sat down opposite Natalie at breakfast. Shredding his croissant anxiously, he asked:

'As Karen is injured, do you fancy skiing with me? There's a quiet area that I discovered last year - it would be perfect for our final morning.'

Natalie had been looking forward to some solo skiing, but she relented.

'OK. Go on, then.'

As soon as she got off the lift she knew. Instead of biting comfortingly into the snow, her skis rattled uncontrollably across the hard packed, glassy surface. Instantly her body reverted to beginner mode. Looking down at the slope as it dropped steeply away, she saw translucent, deadly ice everywhere and fought back tears as Ben joined her.

'Sorry about the ice,' he began. 'The conditions here are different from last year.'

Natalie was frantic.

'I can't do this!'

'Of course, you can. You're just out of your comfort zone. A bit like me, sometimes.'

Natalie stared at him, realisation dawning.

'The secret to skiing on ice is letting go. Don't try and control it – just go with it. Let me show you...'

Natalie took Ben's advice and let go. She fell several times and cursed Ben repeatedly but over the course of the morning, with his help, she mastered the dreaded ice. Smiling with triumphant relief, she finally glided to a halt beside him.

'Well, it seems you're actually good at leaving your comfort zone behind,' smiled Ben. 'Better than me, definitely. Fancy teaching me how?'

This time Natalie did not hesitate.

'Yes,' she replied.

23 IT'S CATCHING

The banner above the stage simply read:

Class of 2029

The stage was empty, as the performance had not yet begun. The audience whispered and giggled, fiddled with their surgical face masks, pawed at their smartphone screens or just stared into space. They were impatient to leave the hall, and the school, behind. Outside, the sun was shining. It was time for life to begin. All that stood between them and their future was one last boring speech.

A diminutive figure strode imperiously across the stage. The hall echoed to the staccato beat of her heels on the wooden floor. When she reached the microphone, the students fell silent. The head teacher nodded; this was the reaction to which she was accustomed.

'Smartphones off – and in your pockets!' she barked. 'My guest did not come all this way for you to play *Contagion* on your phones.'

She waited with folded arms until she was satisfied that all the offending items had been stowed. Then she began.

'Our keynote speaker requires no introduction. Nowadays you all know her name, but once she sat in this hall, just like you. Impatient and anonymous. Desperate to escape these tedious speeches. Then she went out and changed the world. Over the past decade, her medical expertise and tireless dedication to mankind have helped us overcome the series of pandemics that have blighted our planet. As we face a new viral mutation, the deadliest to date, there is no one I would rather have in our corner. What's more, the King clearly agrees with me. That's why, last week, he made her a Dame. Long overdue, in my opinion, but there we are. Women still don't get the recognition they deserve, but I digress. Without further ado, I would like to welcome a former student, of whom we are very proud. Please give a warm welcome to – Dame Rosamund North!'

The head teacher retreated to a chair at the side of the stage, and a blonde woman in jeans and sneakers silently took her place. She removed her hands from her pockets to adjust the microphone, which barely reached her chest. The head teacher sprung to her feet, eager to help, but the woman waved her away.

'I've got this.'

Below, one of the students whispered to his friend:

'She's *hot*.'

'Shut *up*! She's old enough to be your mother. She's got great legs, but no one says, "I've got this" anymore.'

Finally, the microphone was fully extended, and Rosamund was ready to begin.

'Hello, everyone. You're in for a big treat today! I've brought along a brand-new epidemiology research paper, which contains cutting-edge thinking on how to control pandemics...'

Above their masks, the students' eyes widened in horror, and Rosamund smiled.

'Just kidding! You can relax. I'm not going to talk about viruses. You all hear quite enough about them as it is. Instead, I'm going to tell you a story.'

'Once upon a time, an elderly woman was waiting at the bus stop outside her apartment block. She was on her way to the shops, but she never got there. Before the bus arrived, a group of young men appeared from nowhere. They grabbed that frail old lady and flung her to the ground. She tried to hang onto her bag, but they kicked her in the ribs until she loosened her grip, then wrenched it from her hands. Before they ran off, they punched her in the face a couple of times for good measure, to punish her for resisting. The old lady must have passed out after that, as the next thing she remembered was seeing a man's face looking down at her. The man was black. She recalled screaming at him to leave her alone, but he calmly replied that he just wanted to check she was OK. Gently he helped her sit up and supported her while he phoned for an ambulance. Then two of his mates appeared, one of them clutching a brightly coloured shopping bag that clashed with his street clothing.

"We got your bag back, lady — and we made those lowlifes regret getting out of bed this morning."

Then they were gone. She never got a chance to thank them.

Soon after, the ambulance arrived. The

elderly lady spent a night in hospital under observation, then recovered at home, where she thought long and hard about the men who had saved her. Before the attack, it was them she would have feared, rather than those who were actually responsible. All because of the colour of their skin. Eventually she decided to do something about it. She figured the least she could do was adjust her attitude, so she baked a cake and took it round to the Yemeni refugees who had recently moved onto the same landing. Normally she scuttled away, if she saw them in the corridor, but today she was determined to behave better.

She had planned just to give them the cake and then make her escape, but they ushered her into their flat and the wife retreated to the kitchen to make tea. In the living room, a little boy was sitting at the dining table, drawing. With his limited English his father attempted to engage her in conversation.

"You – English?"

"Yes, I am. In fact, I was an English teacher, when I was younger."

The man looked puzzled, so she mimed writing on an imaginary blackboard. "Teacher? Professeur?" She realised it was unlikely he spoke French, but it was the only foreign language she knew.

The man's face lit up. "Mudaris!" He jumped to his feet and rushed into the kitchen, where he spoke excitedly to his wife. Then he returned, sat back down and looked into her eyes.

"Please help – my son. English. Mudaris – you. Please."

The meaning was clear. She was being asked to teach their son English, so he wouldn't be overlooked at school and would have a future. The father had spotted a lifeline, and she was it. Then the mother brought in a pot of fragrant tea, for them to drink with the cake. Catherine took a sip and steadied her nerves.

"Yes. I'll do it. I'll teach your son English." Pointing at her chest, she smiled. "Mudaris.'"

'Fast forward a few years and Jamal is sitting at the living room table with Mrs Baker, his English teacher. He knows her first name is Catherine, but he never calls her that, and she wouldn't like it if he did. It wouldn't be respectful. Mrs Baker is checking his English essay, before he takes it to school to be marked. She isn't pleased.

"Come on, Jamal! You can do better than this. Look – you've used this verb incorrectly. What kind of verb is it?"

"A transitive verb, Mrs Baker."

"And what does a transitive verb do?"

"It takes a direct object."

"Exactly. Change it, please."

"They don't teach us this stuff at school, Mrs Baker."

"I'm well aware of that, Jamal. That's why I'm teaching it to you. It's essential that you get one step ahead and stay that way. You need perfect English if you're going to make it to medical school."

Across the room, Jamal's father smiled as he picked up his teacup.'

'Anatomy classes are different from how they used to be, and that's a good thing. When my parents were medical students, the bodies on which they practised were often treated as playthings. It was a coping strategy, I suppose. In the pub at night, medics would sometimes produce fingers or toes from their pockets, to freak out their mates. If said mates were from the Arts faculty, the trick worked especially well. Nowadays this levity is rightly frowned upon. The good people who donate their bodies to medical schools, to help educate the next cohort of doctors, deserve and receive our deep respect.

However, I could have done with some of

that misplaced humour in my first anatomy class. I had never seen a dead body before, and I didn't react well. In fact, I fainted and was revived by my fellow students. I was so embarrassed and terrified it would happen again. In my second anatomy class, it did. When I recovered, I fled. My confidence was shot. I realised medicine was the wrong career for me, so I made an appointment with my tutor and told him I was quitting.

Spoiler alert – I didn't quit. My tutor was amazing. He gave me a different perspective on my anatomy class, by telling me I should feel privileged, as I was enabling those people to help make a better world after their deaths, just like they wanted. By fainting and then running out on them, I was denying them their destiny. I owed it to them to engage with them, dissect them, study them in minute detail and become the best doctor I could possibly be.

Inspired by his words, I returned to my anatomy class and managed to stay conscious. It was third time lucky, for me. That could have been the end of the story, but afterwards my tutor stuck with me. He constantly looked out for me, throughout my student days and during my gruelling early years as a junior doctor. He is my mentor, my inspiration and my lifelong friend. Whenever my job gets too much, his door is always open. I feel honoured to be godmother to his eldest daughter. He is one of the country's leading public health experts. Some of you might have heard of him. His name is Professor Jamal Mansour.'

'Now I know from experience that many of you won't have been listening that closely. I get that; really I do. The sun is out, and you've got other, more important things to think about, but bear with me. I just need you to pay attention for the final few minutes, while I join the dots, because this is important.

Those anonymous black men rescued Catherine Baker from her assailants and treated her with kindness. As a result, she baked a cake for some Yemeni refugees and agreed to teach English to their son Jamal. Aged eighteen years, a young man with great verbal fluency passed his 'A' Levels and went on to achieve his lifelong ambition of becoming a doctor. After he qualified, he was working as a tutor at a London medical school, when a desperate first year student came to him for help. He responded with the kindness he learned at his living room table, thus saving my career and enabling me to go on and do the stuff I've done, which is probably what you expected me to talk about today. I'm sorry if I've disappointed you. All I'm going to say about my work is — it's my way of being kind to the world.

I could have come here to my old school and told you viruses are contagious, but you already know that. You're all wearing new generation masks. But remember that kindness is contagious too. I want you all to go out there and make kindness go viral as you live your lives. If you do, the world truly will be a better place. With or without masks. Thank you.'

Dame Rosamund North adjusted the microphone to its former height. Then she quietly left the stage.

24 HOME RUN

Calvin sits alone beside the road. The traffic roars past, oblivious. Calvin thinks for a moment and realises there's a simple explanation. After he and Daddy went for a wee, Daddy must have forgotten to put him back in the car. Daddy will remember soon. He'll notice the car's too quiet. If he doesn't, Mummy will. No need to worry.

He waits for ages, but the car doesn't return. It's getting cold. Calvin shivers and concludes that Daddy and Mummy haven't forgotten him, after all. It's his fault for being noisy in the car. They're always telling him off about it. He tries to be quiet, but it's difficult, when he's excited about taking a trip.

Calvin decides to walk home. When he gets

back, maybe Daddy and Mummy won't be angry anymore. Even if they are, perhaps he can calm them down, by being on his best behaviour. Sometimes that works.

He knows busy roads are dangerous. Luckily, there's a wood alongside. Calvin decides to walk through it, in the opposite direction to Daddy's car. He crunches through paper-dry leaves and squelches through mud. The pale evening sunlight intermittently warms his back. There's a tiny shock of cold each time he returns to the shade. He sees signs that others have passed this way. A crisp packet glints, incongruously silver. It's empty, which is a shame, as he's hungry.

Calvin spots an empty glass bottle and recognises the smell rising from its open mouth. When Daddy and Mummy drink from bottles like this, they become even louder than Calvin in the car. At first, they seem happy. Later, they fight. Calvin puts himself to bed, just to avoid them.

The shadows lengthen and the sun slips away. Calvin had hoped to be home for dinner, but the walk is longer than expected. He perseveres, but as the trees and bushes merge into amorphous blackness, he knows it's no use. He'll have to sleep in the woods.

As he curls up small, Calvin feels grateful this happened when he was five. He wouldn't have coped if he were younger.

Calvin wakes early. He's tired, and achy from the damp ground, but he's relieved to discern once again the outlines of the trees. The world smells fresh, yet pungent, as if reborn overnight out of decay. Beyond the wood, the traffic still roars. Calvin stands up and heads for home.

The terrain changes. The ground slopes uphill and the bushes thin out. Calvin spots a gravel path ahead and takes it. He prefers the leafy woodland carpet, but knows gravel means people. Soon he emerges from the wood, blinking in the glare of an open sunlit space. Below is a green swathe, criss-crossed with paths. An oval pond reflects the scudding clouds. Beyond are buildings. Lots of them.

Calvin recognises this place. He dimly remembers Daddy and Mummy bringing him here, but might have doubted himself, were it not for the smell. The all-pervading, wheaten sweetness, exhaled from factory chimneys, convinces him he's home.

A milder version of the smell lives in their kitchen at breakfast. On a good day, Mummy opens the packet, puts two biscuits in her bowl, then adds milk. If Calvin has been good, she puts a biscuit in his bowl. Daddy doesn't like the biscuits. He shouts at Mummy if she serves them to him. He prefers bacon. Calvin does too, but he eats his biscuit to please Mummy. He's desperate to see her.

Calvin charges downhill, towards the town. Soon he's panting for breath but keeps running until he's among the houses. The traffic noise has receded; the roads here are quieter and safer. Unfortunately, they all look the same. So do the houses. Calvin gasps his way down one street, then the next, searching in vain for the rusting, broken pram in his front garden. Eventually exhaustion forces him to stop. His chest heaves as he struggles to recover. Then he hears a voice.

'Calvin? Is that you? What are you doing out this early? I'd better take you home.'

The man scoops Calvin into his arms and strides away briskly. As he turns a corner, Calvin's body floods with relief. There it is, a few houses down. The pram. Calvin squirms and tries to free himself, but the man holds him firm. He walks past the pram and rings the doorbell. After a few seconds, Daddy answers.

'Hello, mate! Is this your Calvin? I found

him wandering the streets. He must have got out.'

Daddy stares at the man, then at Calvin. At that moment Calvin realises he must have done something really naughty, because Daddy doesn't look pleased to see him.

'Yeah, it is – but he didn't get out. We took him to the animal shelter. Missus said we couldn't afford him no more. He must've escaped. Give him 'ere - I'll take him back. Tell 'em to lock him up proper this time.'

'It's alright, pal. I'll take him for you.'

'You sure?'

'Absolutely. No drama. Catch you later.'

Daddy shuts the door, and the man walks away. Calvin wriggles and cries in his arms. The man bends his head and whispers in Calvin's ear:

'Don't fret, little man. I'm not taking you to the shelter. I don't reckon you were there in the first place. Your Dad's not gonna win an Oscar for his acting, is he? Besides, no pets escape from the shelter and even if they did, it's miles away. You'd never have found your way back.'

The man gently strokes Calvin's head.

'My kids have been nagging us for ages to get a dog, so I regard this as a sign. Fancy coming home with me, Calvin? I'll explain to your Dad next time I run into him.'

Calvin falls silent.

'Think you could cope with being spoiled rotten by two little girls?'

Calvin's tail thumps against the man's side.

'I'll take that as a "yes." Come on, then. Let's go home.'

25 THE POWER OF LOVE

Their eyes meet. The seductress raises her glass. Captivated, he approaches.

Later, they kiss their way to his room, where she breaks away, breathless.

'Time out! My battery's dying.'

'I've got a phone charger,' he replies, puzzled.

She lifts her blouse. The socket is embedded in her navel.

'Different kind of charger.'

26 OUT OF THE DARKNESS

Please forgive my errors. Seven thousand languages are spoken on your sphere alone, and millions more across the universe. I can communicate in each one, but occasionally I make mistakes. In fact, I nearly made a fundamental error just now, by claiming that only The One is infallible. That's not true. The One is neither fallible nor infallible. The One just *is*.

Recently The One requested an update on my project, and my first challenge is to explain to you how this happens. To make it relatable to the sentient beings on your sphere, know that I don't receive a knock on my office door nor an email in my inbox. Concepts such as offices, emails and smartphones are exclusive to your sphere and irrelevant to me. What happens is that I gradually become aware of The One's presence within me. It's a little like dreaming, but more tangible; less evanescent. It's akin to being possessed. If you think that sounds terrifying, you're correct. It can be. That's why only the chosen few are able to report directly (is that the correct term?) to The One. I'm privileged to be among them.

My second challenge is to explain my project and its vital importance to your species. I'll start by giving the project a name – although I have no need for such conventions. I note that your business community loves three-letter titles, so let's call it the Sphere Lifecycle Study. Essentially, I monitor every single sphere in the universe. It's not as difficult as it sounds, because the vast majority are devoid of sentient life and are therefore of no interest to me. Should any of these benighted spheres show signs of emerging from The Darkness, I have devised a mechanism that alerts me and brings them within the scope of my project.

The 'Sphere Lifecycle' in the project title is initiated as follows. As a consequence of its position in the universe, a particular sphere begins to be colonised by the most basic life forms. Clearly this has happened on your sphere, as on many others. Gradually, these life forms evolve into myriad organisms and species; some simple, others more sophisticated. Many of the latter acquire the ability to learn, although the rates at which they do so vary immeasurably. The faster these creatures learn, the more rapidly the lifecycle on their particular sphere plays out. You should know that, despite the innumerable varieties of sentient being in the universe, which you could not begin to fathom, the lifecycle followed by their spheres is depressingly similar. Identical, in fact. I shall attempt to describe it to you in the simplest way possible.

At first, the so-called 'intelligent life forms' on the sphere in question aspire only to survive and pass their genes to the next generation. This is Phase One. However, their inherent ambition soon becomes apparent, and they begin to desire and strive for more. In Phase Two, they devise the means to communicate and work in teams to invent devices that remove drudgery and make their lives richer and more rewarding. Sadly, they also learn to misunderstand, mistrust and ultimately hate each other. Their intelligence and ingenuity enable them to come up with ways to punish and ultimately destroy those they hate, and to retaliate against supposed or actual wrongs visited upon them. It is this hatred that inevitably leads them into Phase Three, the endgame, where they self-destruct and return their sphere to The Darkness whence it came.

I am conscious that, when I use words like 'rates' and 'rapidly,' you will inevitably infer the concept of time and associate it with the lifecycle of the spheres. It is difficult for you to avoid doing this, but I urge you to try, because time does not exist. The sentient beings on your sphere – and others – invented it, in order to try and make sense of their worlds, but it is meaningless to me, and to The One. I know that many of you can feel this if you make the space in your soul – but I digress.

The main point I seek to convey is that the Sphere Lifecycle is not inevitable. Know that it was intended by The One as a challenge; a kind of assault course, if you will. That's why the Sphere Lifecyle Study was created. The purpose of my project, the most important project ever conceived, is to identify those spheres which are able to resist The Darkness and discover how to live in true harmony with the universe. The trouble is, I have not yet identified a single one. Each and every 'sentient sphere' has self-destructed before it could discover its true purpose, and The One is losing patience. If I don't come up with a success story soon, a central design principle of the universe – Free Will – risks being revoked, and the consequences for the inhabitants of spheres like yours would be deeply unpleasant.

Happily, all is not lost. Some spheres are populated by highly evolved life forms which are within reach of their true purpose. Yours is one of them. You have the potential to discover your truth before you implode. However, it will not be easy. Most of your inhabitants are still imbued with The Darkness from which they evolved, but this can be overcome.

I should leave you to scale the remaining obstacles on your own, as I am not supposed to interfere, but I have concluded that you need help. I therefore offer my assistance – but be warned. If you choose to take it, the path will not be easy. Before the process is complete, you will undoubtedly wish that you had chosen The Darkness, so think carefully about whether your sphere is up to the challenge. I will wait with interest to see whether you – and the other spheres to whom I have extended the same offer – will accept.

If you do, and if, more importantly, you succeed, you will share the ultimate reward.

Over to you.

27 REDUCED CIRCUMSTANCES

Every morning Maria awoke to a stunning view of Schönbrunn Palace, the Versailles of Austria. The first thing she did each day was admire its mustard yellow façade and ornate gardens, but today something was amiss. Slowly Maria got to her feet and took three tentative steps forward. She reached up and carefully straightened the picture in its antique wooden frame, then removed a handkerchief from the pocket of her nightdress and wiped away a few specks of dust. She couldn't let the palace look shabby; that would never do.

Dust rarely had a chance to settle in Maria's little bedsit, where an orderly routine was scrupulously maintained. The bed was left to air for exactly fifteen minutes, then made with a precision taught by her mother, many decades ago. Maria still slept under blankets and starched white cotton sheets. She was suspicious of duvets which, in her opinion, were for people with sloppy habits. It was quite evident that her next-door neighbour Liesl had a duvet, as did most of the occupants of her apartment block.

Right on cue, she heard Liesl's front door open. There was a brief, whispered conversation, then the sound of footsteps echoed around the corridor outside, gradually receding as Liesl's last customer departed. While Maria boiled the kettle for breakfast, she reflected that he must have more money than some; she knew Liesl charged extra for an overnight stay.

Breakfast was tea, served from a pewter teapot, with a single slice of toast. Maria didn't take milk; in her opinion it spoiled the fragrance of the tea and anyway, milk always went off before she had a chance to drink it all. She spread some cherry jam on her toast, then left most of it and scraped the contents of her plate carefully into the kitchen bin. Her appetite wasn't what it used to be.

Time for a bath. Maria reached into the space under the kitchen sink and, after several attempts, dragged out a small bathtub. At a pinch, she could have manoeuvred her delicate frame into a seated position, but she preferred to wash standing up. It was so much easier. She took hold of the extendable shower head, positioned between the kitchen taps, and removed her bar of lavender soap from the soap dish on the draining board. While washing, she took care not to soak the kitchen floor and to use the minimum amount of water. People were so wasteful, these days. As she dried herself, she was pleased to see that only a few drops of water had escaped the confines of the tub and fallen on the ancient, discoloured floor tiles. She mopped them up immediately, so as not to slip.

Maria made few concessions to vanity, but she always took care to use a high-quality face cream, just like her mother used to do. She looked in the mirror as she applied the cream and regarded with equanimity the many wrinkles that had appeared over the years, despite her daily skincare routine. Her face might be weathered and lined, but she knew it had been loved. Maria smiled to herself as names and faces from the past floated back to her. In their memory, she would always take care to look smart and presentable. In a way, she felt she owed it to them.

Today was a special day, so it was

particularly important to look her best. From her narrow wardrobe Maria extracted one of her two remaining designer dresses; old-fashioned, but beautifully tailored and lined with cool, turquoise silk that was almost intact. After she had put it on, she twisted her iron-grey hair into a neat chignon and fixed it in place with a tortoiseshell comb. She hoped that the man who had sent the letter would appreciate the effort she had made.

Maria sat down at the small table, pushed up against the wall to make best use of the limited space and covered with one of her embroidered tablecloths, to hide the burn marks and stains left by previous occupants. Carefully she opened the envelope, which was already showing signs of wear and tear from having been handled countless times before, and extracted the letter. The weight and quality of the cream-coloured paper pleased her; people rarely used good writing materials, these days. In fact, hardly anyone took the trouble to write letters at all.

The letter was concise. The man, whose name Maria didn't recognise, simply requested the pleasure of her company at Demel, located inside the Ringstrasse in Vienna's exclusive first district. Clearly he knew enough about her to suggest meeting at her favourite coffee shop - if she dared to demean Demel with such a term. For this reason alone, Maria intended to return to a place she hadn't visited for many years, even though the journey would require some effort.

An hour before the appointed time, Maria locked the door of her bedsit behind her and walked down the corridor whose greasy, sage green tiles always made her feel slightly queasy, as did the malodorous shared toilet she used as infrequently as possible. Once in the lobby, she checked her post-box, which contained the usual leaflets advertising local pizza parlours, nightclubs and sex shops. The last letter she had received was already tucked safely in her handbag.

Slowly Maria made her way down Hoffmangasse, her gait upright and elegant despite her age and her stubborn refusal to use a stick. Only occasionally did she need to pause and rest her hand briefly against the wall. Eventually she reached the tram stop on the Gürtel, Vienna's outer ring road; the cacophonous, disreputable cousin of the genteel, refined Ringstrasse to which tram number forty-two would transport her.

The tram rattled its way past the Volksoper, the people's opera house that resembled an old-fashioned wedding cake and was rarely visited by tourists, unlike its famous counterpart on the Ring. Ahead lay the seemingly endless Währingerstrasse. Maria listened to the monotone recording that told passengers the name of each upcoming stop and where they could change onto the different tram and bus routes. The announcer displayed all the enthusiasm of a corpse. Maria wondered why he had been selected, when there were so many great performers living in the city. Undoubtedly it had something to do with money. She contemplated the grand houses on either side of the street and their long-departed occupants, some of whom she had known. Most of the houses had been converted into apartments or offices. No one lived in big houses like that anymore. Eventually the twin spires of the Votivkirche pierced the sky on her right-hand side and she heard the name of the final stop.

As the tram approached Schottentor it abruptly disappeared underground, circling into the concrete depths like a fairground ride, before coming to a halt. Maria climbed carefully down the steps. Once she would have walked to Demel from here in just a few minutes, striding out in cheerful anticipation of 'Kaffee und Kuchen,' but those days were gone. Instead, she transferred onto Tram D, alighting near the sprawling Hofburg Palace. She briefly admired its imposing exterior, then slowly made her way around to the back and began negotiating the narrow streets of the first district, with their opulent shopfronts and long-held secrets. Even after so many years living in the eighteenth district, with its seedy sex shops and sordid reputation, the first district was still where she felt most at home.

Maria arrived slightly early at the gilded, sumptuous temple to confectionery indulgence known to the locals as 'Der Demel.' A waitress wearing a severe black dress and a starched white apron showed her to the table for two that she requested. A few minutes later the waitress returned.

'Haben Sie schon gewählt, gnädige Frau?'

Her polite, but rather archaic choice of words pleased Maria, who replied that she would prefer to wait until her companion arrived.

She didn't notice him approach; he must have done so quietly. Suddenly, there he was. Tall, thin and slightly stooped, smartly dressed in a sports jacket and chinos, his white hair brushed back neatly from his high patrician forehead.

Maria started struggling to her feet, but the man motioned for her to remain in her seat.

'Fürstin. Please, don't get up.'

The man's accent was a surprise to Maria; she thought it seemed at odds with his appearance. He waved his hand imperiously and the waitress returned to take their order. Sachertorte, the tourist's favourite, for him, accompanied by a milky Wiener Melange. Maria requested a black coffee and a slice of strudel. They both remained silent until the waitress was out of earshot.

'Fürstin?'

Maria raised her eyebrows.

'No one has called me "Princess" for many years. It's actually illegal to do so, here in Austria. Did you know that?'

'I doubt the Polizei will arrest me,' the man replied. 'Anyway, where I come from, people are allowed to use their titles, so to me you are Fürstin Maria von Edelstein, just as I wrote on the envelope. We've been trying to find you for many years, your Royal Highness.'

'I suppose you didn't expect a princess to be living in the eighteenth district,' Maria observed with a wry smile. 'My family had to sell what remained of our land and property for tax and – other reasons. My father made some poor business decisions, as did my late husband. So, the eighteenth is where I am spending my twilight years.'

'Not necessarily.'

The man leaned forward and rested his elbows on the table. Two elderly ladies at the next table regarded him with disapproval. Oblivious, he explained to Maria about the other branch of the family living in the United States, where they had emigrated just before the Anschluss. Her father and his closest relatives had apparently elected to remain in Austria. Maria said she never realised they had a choice, and briefly contemplated the consequences of that decision, which had reverberated across the subsequent decades. Then the man told her how he, his wife and daughters were constantly researching their family history and looking for relatives in Europe who were still alive, particularly those in what he called "reduced circumstances." He proudly announced that they would be honoured to offer her a home in Ohio, a ready-made family and a lifestyle that, whilst not luxurious, would be far better suited to a princess than her current existence. Maria toyed with her strudel and said nothing.

Later that evening, Maria sat at the table in her bedsit with a glass of Gemischter Salz, the local wine that was her only other concession to luxury, apart from her face cream. As she sipped her wine, she reflected on her decision. She was sure it was the right one. After all, she had lived in this building for so long and had got used to it, like a shoe that pinched at first but gradually became comfortable, without the wearer really noticing. There could be no doubt; she had definitely made the sensible choice.

For the first time in years, Maria broke one of her self-imposed rules and allowed herself a second glass of wine, meaning that she stayed up later than normal; late enough to hear Liesl open her front door to greet her first customer of the evening. Smiling just a little, Maria undid the clasp of her battered leather handbag and looked inside. There it still was - tucked away among the pizza parlour, nightclub and sex shop leaflets she had extracted from her mailbox earlier. An open plane ticket to Columbus. Maria made a mental note not to throw it away by accident when she put the leaflets in the bin.

28 LUCKY ESCAPE

She soaks her feet in hot water until they swell.

She hears the knock at the door, her sisters' disappointed cries, then footsteps on the scullery stairs.

'Shame,' the prince sighs. 'Doesn't fit.'

Afterwards, she runs to the stables.

'Let's go!'

'Cinderella,' cries the stable boy. 'I thought you'd never ask!'

29 THE DAY THE MUSIC NEARLY DIED

Pete loved to play tricks on his mother. It was the only way to get her attention. The Casbah Coffee Club, which she ran from their cellar, took up most of her time and energy. There was little left for her troubled son, with his dreams of fame and fortune.

Tonight, Mum was at the stove with her back to him, oblivious. As Pete walked past, on his way out, the opportunity was too good to miss. He slid quietly through the kitchen doorway and shouted:

'Boo!'

Three things happened at once. Mum screamed, her slippered feet left the ground and a glistening arc of boiling oil flew backwards across the kitchen, narrowly missing her son.

'Pete – what the hell were you thinking! I could have killed you – are you alright?'

'Yeah – just caught a few drops.'

Pete held out his arm, on which a constellation of burns glowed an angry red.

'Run it under the cold tap. God, look at this mess.'

Hands on hips, Mum surveyed her kitchen wall, whose turquoise emulsion was greedily soaking up the grease, spreading the stain relentlessly in all directions.

'Sorry, Mum. I didn't think…'

'Too right you didn't!'

'I'll clear it up, I promise…'

'Leave it. You'd only make it worse. Put some Savlon on those burns, then get out of my sight.'

'I've got band practice, so I'll be home late…'

'Just as well. Now go!'

Pete escaped into the dark and stormy night.

In a smarter house nearby, absorbed in his writing, Paul hunched over his desk in a bay window overlooking the garden. He scrutinised five variations of the same line, then obliterated each one with a vicious swipe of his pen. Then he pushed back his chair and ran his hands through his hair in frustration.

Suddenly the bay window imploded, showering the room with glass confetti. Paul toppled backwards and cracked his head on the parquet floor. Dazed, he struggled upright and stared in disbelief at the huge tree branch on his desk, right where his head had been bent over his lyrics just seconds earlier.

Paul's father rushed into the room.

'What's going on? Jesus - are you OK, son?'

'Yes, I'm fine.'

Paul quickly remembered his priorities.

'Dad – do you need help getting the window fixed? It's just that I've got band practice soon…'

'OK – you go ahead. I'll call a glazier and sort this out.'

'Thanks, Dad. Leave the sweeping up to me. I'll do it when I get back.'

John was sorry he had forgotten his hat. The rain saturated his hair and water droplets traced a remorseless path down his back, inside his sodden jumper. He considered holding his guitar case over his head but rejected the idea. It just wouldn't look cool.

A gang of lads emerged from a pub and headed in John's direction on unsteady feet. They shoved each other playfully, struggled to light their cigarettes and took ownership of the pavement. Clearly, they weren't going to move for anyone, especially a skinny dude in a rain mac, clutching a guitar.

John considered taking them on but decided against it. Instead, he faced them down until the last moment, then stepped off the pavement. The roaring wind drowned out the engine of the car right behind him, but the blare of the horn and the squeal of swerving tyres told him it had been a close call.

Predictably, the gang cracked up, but the adrenaline spike from John's brush with death gave him the courage to answer back.

'Laugh it up, boys! I could have been killed!'

The gang was unimpressed.

'Ooh, he could have been killed. Imagine that...' one of them sniggered.

'Yeah, just imagine...' added his mate.

They continued to laugh as they walked away.

George's mother looked up wearily from the ironing board. Her lacquered curls clung damply to her forehead.

'When are you going to get a proper job and bring home a decent wage, instead of poncing around with your stupid friends?'

'We've been through this, Mother. The band's going places. It won't be long before we make it big…'

'Pipe dreams don't put food on the table, George. I want you down the Labour Exchange tomorrow.'

'Just have a little patience, Ma. You don't understand how these things work…'

'Oh, so I'm stupid, now?'

Mother's voice grew louder and shriller.

'I never said that. Look, I've got to go. It's band practice tonight…'

'I might have known!' shrieked Mother. 'You and that bloody band…'

The red mist descended without warning. With a deft flick of her left wrist, Mother yanked the plug from its socket, then used her right hand to launch the searing hot iron at her son's head as he opened the lounge door. George felt its heat as it sailed past his cheek and hit the wall, where it gouged a hole in the plaster and left a burn mark on the wallpaper. Quickly he slipped through the door and closed it behind him.

'So, let's get this straight,' said John. 'Your

mum nearly fried you like a chip, Pete; meanwhile George almost got brained by *his* mum, with the iron. You both want to remember that, on Mother's Day. Then I too have a close call, thanks to a speeding car, and Paul here just misses being flattened by a falling tree.'

'It has got to be a sign,' observed Paul. 'I mean, that we should rename the band in honour of our four accidents, which could have been much worse. Maybe call ourselves "Charmed Life" - or something like that.'

'Sounds like a bunch of pretentious art school students,' Pete grumbled. 'How about "Near Miss" instead?'

'It's better than the name we've got now, but it won't work,' declared John. 'Whatever we call ourselves, it still has to start with "The" - like all the best bands. We have to call ourselves "The – Something." We just need to decide on the second word.'

'I'm sure we can work it out,' said Paul.

ABOUT THE AUTHOR

Felicity Radcliffe divides her time between a small rural village, where she lives with her husband and dog, and a narrowboat on England's beautiful canals. Ice Magic is her first anthology.

Felicity is also the author of the Grand Union series – a trilogy of crime mysteries set on the canal network.

MORE FREE STUFF…

Hello - thank you so much for reading Ice Magic. As with the Grand Union series, I'd love to know what you thought of it. I'm currently working on my next novel, so any feedback would be very helpful.

Please email me at **felicityradcliffebooks@gmail.com** to start our conversation. Alternatively, you can contact me via Facebook, Twitter or Instagram. Writing is a solitary process and I do get quite lonely at times, so it would be great to hear from you.

If you join my mailing list, I'll share a whole load of free stuff with you. I regularly send out short stories and poems, and I'll make sure you get a copy of each one.

If you have enjoyed reading this book, please tell your friends and ask them to contact me. It makes my day when someone tells me that a friend recommended my books. It also gives me a boost when I receive reviews on Amazon, Goodreads and Bookbub, so please do leave me a review for Ice Magic. Whatever rating you choose to give, I value your opinion.

I look forward to hearing from you. Thanks again for choosing Ice Magic and, if you haven't already done so, please check out my Grand Union series. You don't have to be a canal enthusiast to enjoy it!

Felicity Radcliffe
December 2023

Printed in Great Britain
by Amazon

33747217R00128